PENGUIN CLASSICS

*Maigret and the Wine Merc*

'I love reading Simenon. He mak
— William Faulkner

'A truly wonderful writer . . . marvellously readable – lucid,
simple, absolutely in tune with the world he creates'
— Muriel Spark

'Few writers have ever conveyed with such a sure touch, the
bleakness of human life'
— A. N. Wilson

'One of the greatest writers of the twentieth century . . .
Simenon was unequalled at making us look inside, though
the ability was masked by his brilliance at absorbing us
obsessively in his stories'
— *Guardian*

'A novelist who entered his fictional world as if he were part
of it'
— Peter Ackroyd

'The greatest of all, the most genuine novelist we have had
in literature'
— André Gide

'Superb . . . The most addictive of writers . . . A unique teller
of tales'
— *Observer*

'The mysteries of the human personality are revealed in all
their disconcerting complexity'
— Anita Brookner

'A writer who, more than any other crime novelist, combined
a high literary reputation with popular appeal'  — P. D. James

'A supreme writer . . . Unforgettable vividness'  — *Independent*

'Compelling, remorseless, brilliant'
— John Gray

'Extraordinary masterpieces of the twentieth century'
— John Banville

# GEORGES SIMENON

# Maigret and the Wine Merchant

Translated by ROS SCHWARTZ

PENGUIN BOOKS

PENGUIN CLASSICS

UK | USA | Canada | Ireland | Australia
India | New Zealand | South Africa

Penguin Books is part of the Penguin Random House group of companies
whose addresses can be found at global.penguinrandomhouse.com.

First published in French as *Maigret et le marchand de vin* by Presses de la Cité 1970
This translation first published 2019
001

Set in 12.5/15 pt Dante MT Std
Typeset by Jouve (UK), Milton Keynes
Printed and bound in Great Britain by Clays Ltd, Elcograf S.p.A.

ISBN: 978-0-241-30428-0

www.greenpenguin.co.uk

MIX
Paper from
responsible sources
FSC® C018179

Penguin Random House is committed to a
sustainable future for our business, our readers
and our planet. This book is made from Forest
Stewardship Council® certified paper.

*Maigret and the Wine Merchant*

# 1.

'You killed her to rob her, didn't you?'

'I didn't want to kill her. The proof is, I only had a toy gun.'

'You knew she had a lot of money?'

'I didn't know how much. She'd worked all her life so by the age of eighty-two or eighty-three, she must have had savings.'

'How many times did you go and ask her for money?'

'I don't know. A few times. When I came to see her, she knew why I was there. She was my grandmother and would always give me five francs. Just think what you can do with five francs when you're unemployed.'

Maigret was solemn and brooding, a little sad. It was a mundane case, a sordid crime of the kind committed almost every week: a boy still in his teens who mugs an elderly woman living alone to fleece her. The difference with Théo Stiernet was that he'd attacked his grandmother.

The boy was much calmer than expected and he answered the questions as best he could. He was a slightly chubby, listless boy, with a round face, almost no chin, bulging eyes and thick lips, so red that at first glance he appeared to be wearing lipstick.

'Five francs, the same as a kid coming to get his weekly pocket money!'

'Is her husband dead?'

'He died nearly forty years ago. She ran a little

haberdashery in Place Saint-Paul for ages. It's only in the past two years that she's had difficulty walking and had to give up the shop.'

'What about your father?'

'He's in the nut house at Bicêtre.'

'Is your mother still around?'

'I haven't lived with her for a long time. She's always drunk.'

'Do you have any brothers or sisters?'

'I've got a sister. She left home at fifteen and no one knows what became of her.'

He spoke without emotion.

'How did you know that your grandmother kept her money in her apartment?'

'She didn't trust banks, not even the Savings Bank.'

It was nine o'clock. The murder had been committed the previous evening at the same hour. It had taken place in the old building in Rue du Roi-de-Sicile, where Joséphine Ménard lived in a one-bedroom apartment on the third floor. A resident from the fourth floor had passed Stiernet on the stairs as he was leaving his grandmother's. She knew him well, and they'd greeted one another.

At around 9.30, another neighbour, Madame Palloc, who lived in the apartment opposite, had dropped by for a chat with the old woman, as she often did.

She knocked, but there was no reply. The door wasn't locked and she turned the handle. Joséphine Ménard was dead, huddled on the floor, her skull split open, her face a pulp.

By six o'clock in the morning, Théo Stiernet had already been found on a bench at the Gare du Nord, where he was sleeping.

'What gave you the idea of killing her?'

'I didn't mean to. She attacked me and I was frightened.'

'You threatened her with your toy gun?'

'Yes. She didn't bat an eyelid. Maybe she saw straight away that it was only a toy.

' "Get out of here, you thug!" she said. "If you think I'm afraid of you . . ."

'She grabbed the scissors from the round table and came towards me, repeating: "Go away . . .! Go away, I say, otherwise you'll be sorry for the rest of your life . . ."

'She was tiny and she seemed frail, but she was very energetic.

'I panicked. I thought she was going to gouge my eyes out with those open scissors. I looked around for something to defend myself with. Next to the stove, there was a poker and I grabbed it.'

'How many times did you hit her?'

'I don't know. She wouldn't fall down. She carried on staring straight at me.'

'Was her face bloody?'

'Yes. I didn't want her to suffer. I don't know. I carried on hitting her.'

Maigret thought he could hear the assistant public prosecutor, in court, saying: *Stiernet then launched into a savage attack against his unfortunate victim . . .*

'What about when she collapsed?'

'I looked at her and I couldn't take in what had happened. I didn't want to kill her. I swear. You can believe me.'

'But you remained cool-headed enough to search the drawers.'

'Not straight away. At first I walked towards the door. Then I remembered that I only had one franc fifty left in my pocket and that I'd been thrown out of my lodgings because I owed three weeks' rent.'

'So you retraced your steps?'

'Yes. I didn't search the apartment as you seemed to be saying. I just opened a few drawers. I found an old purse which I slipped into my pocket. Then I came across a cardboard box containing two rings and a cameo brooch.'

These items were on Maigret's desk, by his pipes, and so was the worn purse.

'You didn't discover her stash?'

'I didn't look for it. I was in a hurry to get out of there, away from the sight of her. Wherever I was in the room, she still seemed to be staring at me. On the stairs, I passed Madame Menou. I went into a bar and drank a brandy. Then, seeing as there were sandwiches on the counter, I ate three.'

'Were you hungry?'

'I suppose so. I ate, I drank a coffee, then I started wandering through the streets. I wasn't much better off than before, because there was only eight francs twenty-five in the purse.'

*I wasn't much better off than before!*

He had said that as if it were the most natural thing in the world and Maigret, pensive, couldn't take his eyes off his face.

'Why did you choose the Gare du Nord?'

'I didn't choose it. I ended up there by chance. It was very cold out.'

This was the 15th of December. The chill wind sprinkled tiny snowflakes on to the cobblestones like dust.

'Did you want to get to Belgium?'

'With the few francs I had left?'

'What were your plans?'

'First of all, to sleep.'

'Did it occur to you that you'd be arrested?'

'I didn't think about it.'

'What did you think about?'

'Nothing.'

In fact, the police had found the hoard of money: twenty-two thousand francs wrapped in packaging paper on top of his grandmother's wardrobe.

'What would you have done if you'd discovered the money?'

'I don't know.'

The door opened and Lapointe came into the office.

'Inspector Fourquet has just phoned. He wanted to speak to you, but I told him you were busy.'

Fourquet belonged to the seventeenth arrondissement, a very bourgeois, wealthy neighbourhood where murders were rare.

'A man has been killed in Rue Fortuny, two hundred metres from the Parc Monceau. From his ID, it seems he's quite a big shot, an important wine wholesaler.'

'Is that all that's known?'

'Apparently he was walking to his car when he was hit by four bullets. There were no witnesses. It's not a busy street and, at that moment, there was no one about.'

Maigret's gaze fell on Stiernet and he shrugged.

'Is Lucas here?'

He went over to the door and spotted Lucas at his desk.

'Would you come in for a minute?'

Stiernet's round eyes went from one to the other as if none of this concerned him.

'Question him again from the beginning and write down his answers. Then have him sign the statement and take him down to the cells. You, Lapointe, come with me.'

He put on his heavy black overcoat and wound the navy-blue wool scarf knitted by Madame Maigret around his neck. Before going out, he filled a fresh pipe, which he lit in the corridor, after a last glance at the murderer.

Although it wasn't that late, there were few people out and about because of the icy wind that stung faces and blew straight through the thickest clothes. The two men clambered into one of the little black cars belonging to the Police Judiciaire and drove to the other side of Paris in record time.

In Rue Fortuny, officers were stopping traffic and preventing curious bystanders from approaching the body, which could be seen lying on the pavement. Four or five men were coming and going around it.

Fourquet was there and stepped forwards to meet Maigret.

'The neighbourhood chief inspector has just arrived, and so has the doctor.'

Maigret already knew the chief inspector well and he shook his hand. He was an elegant, pleasant man.

'Do you know Oscar Chabut?'

'Should I know him?'

'He's quite an important man, one of the biggest wine merchants in Paris: Le Vin des Moines. You'll have seen the name on lorries and posters. He has barges on the river and railway tank-wagons.'

The man lying on the pavement was corpulent but not

fat. He had the build of a rugby player. The doctor had stood up and was dusting down the knees of his trousers, which were covered in powdery snow.

'He couldn't have survived more than two or three minutes. The autopsy will tell us more.'

Maigret looked at the very light-blue, almost grey, staring eyes, the craggy face with a solid jaw that was beginning to sag.

The van with the team from Criminal Records pulled up by the kerb and the forensic experts brought out their equipment, as a film or television crew would.

'Have you informed the prosecutor's office?'

'Yes. He's going to send a deputy and an examining magistrate.'

Maigret looked around for Fourquet and spied him a few paces away, his long arms wrapped around his body in an attempt to keep warm.

'Which is his car?'

There were five or six parked by the kerb, all expensive models. Chabut's was a red Jaguar.

'Have you searched the glove box?'

'Yes. Sunglasses, a Michelin Guide, two road maps of Provence and a packet of cough pastilles.'

'It's almost certain he had just come out of a building in this street.'

Rue Fortuny wasn't very long and, on turning round, Maigret recognized the private mansion in front of which the body still lay. It was a 1900s-style house, with ornate carved stonework around the windows. He thought he saw the cover of the spyhole in the studded oak door move.

'Come with me, Lapointe . . .'

He walked over to the doorstep and pressed the bell. It was some time before the door opened. A woman stood in the unlit entrance hall, half of her face and one shoulder visible from the outside.

'What is it?'

Maigret knew who she was.

'Good evening, Blanche.'

'What do you want of me?'

'Detective Chief Inspector Maigret. Don't you remember? Admittedly, it's a good ten years since we last saw each other.'

He pushed open the door without being invited in.

'Come in,' he said to Lapointe. 'You're too young to have known Madame Blanche, as everyone calls her.'

As if he was already in familiar surroundings, Maigret turned the light switch and pushed one of the double doors that opened into a vast lounge. It was full of carpets and wall hangings, multicoloured cushions and lamps with silk shades giving out a soft glow.

Madame Blanche looked around fifty but she must have been sixty. She was a plump little woman whom some would have found very distinguished. She was wearing a black silk dress and a triple-strand pearl necklace that stood out in striking contrast.

'As active and as discreet as ever?'

He'd first met her thirty years earlier, when she was still a streetwalker on Boulevard de la Madeleine. She was pretty and sweet, and always had a friendly smile that gave her two dimples.

Later, she became a madam's assistant in an apartment

in Rue Notre-Dame-de-Lorette, where clients could be assured of meeting pretty women.

She had come up in the world. Now she was the owner of this private residence offering lovers an elegant, luxurious hideaway and the best brands of champagne and whisky.

'What happened?' asked Maigret while she composed herself.

'Nothing happened here. I don't know what went on outside. I noticed some to-ing and fro-ing.'

'You didn't hear any shots?'

'Were they shots? I thought it was a car backfiring.'

'Where were you?'

'To tell you the truth, I'd just finished eating in the kitchen. Just a little slice of bread and some ham. I never have dinner.'

'Who is in the house?'

'No one. Why?'

'Who was Oscar Chabut with?'

'Who is Oscar Chabut?'

'You had better cooperate, otherwise I'll have to take you to Quai des Orfèvres.'

'I only know my clients by their first names. They are nearly all important people.'

'And you only open the door a fraction after looking at them through the spyhole.'

'This is a respectable establishment. I don't accept just anyone. That's why the Vice Squad leaves us in peace.'

'Did you also look through the spyhole when Chabut left?'

'What makes you think that?'

'Lapointe, drive her to Quai des Orfèvres, where she might be a bit more talkative.'

'I can't leave here. I'll tell you what I know. I presume this Chabut is the client who left around half an hour ago.'

'Is he a regular? Did he come here often?'

'From time to time.'

'Once a month? Once a week?'

'More like weekly.'

'Always with the same person?'

'No, not always.'

'Was his companion today a new one?'

She hesitated and eventually shrugged.

'I don't see why I should get myself into hot water. She's been here around thirty times over the past year.'

'Did he telephone you to tell you he was coming?'

'As they all do.'

'What time did they get here?'

'Around seven.'

'Together, or separately?'

'Together. I recognized the red car straight away.'

'Did they order anything to drink?'

'The champagne was waiting for them in an ice bucket.'

'Where is the woman?'

'But . . . She left—'

'After Chabut was shot?'

He caught a flicker of indecision in her eyes.

'Of course not.'

'You claim she left first?'

'She did, that's a fact.'

'I don't believe you, Blanche.'

He had often had to deal with establishments of this

kind in the course of his career and was familiar with their ways. So he knew it was always the man who left first, giving his companion time to freshen up.

'Show me to the room they used. Lapointe, you watch the corridor and make sure no one leaves. Now, where were they?'

'On the first floor. The pink room.'

The walls were panelled, the bannister rail carved. The carpet underfoot, secured by brass stair-rods, was pale blue and soft.

'When I saw you turn up—'

'Because you were watching through the spyhole?'

'That's only natural, isn't it? I wanted to find out what was going on. When I recognized you, I guessed at once that it spelled trouble for me—'

'Admit you knew his name.'

'Yes.'

'And that of his companion?'

'Only her first name, I swear. Anne-Marie. They call her the Grasshopper.'

'Why?'

'Because she's tall and skinny, with long legs and long arms.'

'Where is she?'

'I told you, she left first.'

'And I don't believe you.'

She pushed open a door into a secluded room where a maid could be seen changing the sheets of a four-poster bed. On a pedestal table was a champagne bottle and two glasses, one of which had lipstick marks and still contained some liquid.

'You can see for yourself that—'

'That she's neither in this room nor in the bathroom. That is correct. How many other rooms do you have?'

'Eight.'

'Are some of them occupied?'

'No. My clients arrive mainly towards the end of the day or much later. I was expecting one at nine o'clock. He must have seen a crowd of people in the street and—'

'Show me the other rooms.'

There were four on the first floor, all in nineteenth-century style, with heavy furniture and a profusion of hangings in faded colours.

'You can see there's no one here.'

'Let us continue.'

'Why would she have gone to the top floor?'

'Let me see it anyway.'

The first two rooms were indeed empty, but in the third a young woman was sitting bolt upright on a garnet-coloured padded velvet chair.

She sprang up. She was tall and slim, with almost no bust or hips.

'Who is she?' asked Maigret.

'She's the girl who was waiting for the nine o'clock client.'

'Do you know her?'

'No.'

But the girl shrugged. She looked under twenty, and now there was a couldn't-care-less attitude about her.

'He'll find out in the end. He's a policeman, isn't he?'

'Detective Chief Inspector Maigret.'

'No kidding?'

She gazed at him with curiosity.

'Are you handling this case personally?'

'As you can see.'

'Is he dead?'

'Yes.'

She turned towards Madame Blanche and said reproachfully:

'Why did you lie to me and say he was only wounded?'

'I couldn't tell. I didn't get anywhere near him.'

'Who are you, mademoiselle?'

'Anne-Marie Boutin. I'm his private secretary.'

'Did you often come here with him?'

'Around once a week. Always on a Wednesday, because that's the day I'm supposed to have an English lesson.'

'Let's go downstairs,' grunted Maigret.

He was a little nauseated by all the pastel tones and soft lighting that made people's faces look a little blurred.

They had stopped in the lounge, but no one had sat down. Voices could be heard, comings and goings outside in the street where the icy wind was blustering, whereas indoors it was too hot, as in a glasshouse. As in a glasshouse too, there were giant plants in Chinese vases.

'What do you know about your boss's murder?'

'What she told me,' replied the Grasshopper, pointing to Madame Blanche. 'That someone shot him and wounded him. That the concierge from next door went out and probably phoned the police, because they turned up within a few minutes.'

The police station was just around the corner, in Avenue de Villiers.

'Did he die more or less straight away?'

'Yes.'

He thought she turned a little paler, but she didn't cry. It was as if she had merely received a shock. She went on flatly:

'I wanted to leave right away, but she wouldn't let me.'

'Why not?' Maigret asked Madame Blanche.

'She'd have walked into the arms of your colleague, who'd just arrived. I'd rather keep her and my establishment out of all this. If the newspapers get wind of it, it will almost certainly get us closed down.'

'Tell me exactly what you saw. Where was the man who shot him?'

'Between two cars, just opposite the front door.'

'Did you get a good look at him?'

'No. The lamp post is quite a long way away. I could only see an outline.'

'Was he tall?'

'More on the short side, broad shoulders, dark clothes. He fired three or four times, I didn't count. Monsieur Oscar clutched his stomach, staggered for a moment and then fell on his face.'

Maigret watched the young woman, who was upset but did not appear distraught.

'Did you love him?'

'What do you mean?'

'How long had you been his mistress?'

She looked taken aback at the word.

'It wasn't quite what you think. He let me know when he wanted me, but he never spoke of love. I didn't think of him as a lover . . .'

'What time is your mother expecting you home?'

'Between half past nine and ten.'

'Where do you live?'

'Rue Caulaincourt, near Place Constantin-Pecqueur.'

'Where are Oscar Chabut's offices?'

'Quai de Charenton, after the Bercy warehouses.'

'Will you be there tomorrow morning?'

'Definitely.'

'I may need you. Lapointe, go out with her and walk her to the Métro, so that if the press has already been alerted, she won't be harassed.'

He fiddled with his pipe as if he was hesitant to fill it and light it in these surroundings. In the end he decided to do so.

Madame Blanche had her hands folded over her podgy stomach and looked at him calmly, with the air of someone who has a clear conscience.

'Are you sure you didn't recognize the shooter?'

'I swear.'

'Did your client sometimes come with married women?'

'I suppose so.'

'Was he a frequent visitor?'

'Sometimes I'd see him several times in the same week, then I'd hear nothing from him for ten days or two weeks. That was rare.'

'No one telephoned you about him?'

'No.'

The deputy prosecutor and the examining magistrate had left. The chill was even more biting than earlier and the men from the Forensic Institute, who had put the wine merchant's body on a stretcher, were heaving it into the van.

The experts from Criminal Records were getting back into their van too.

'Have you found anything?'

'The cartridge cases. Four. 6.35 calibre.'

A small calibre. An amateur or a woman's gun, which had to be fired at close range.

'No reporters?'

'Two came. They left quite quickly so as not to miss the deadline for their local editions.'

Inspector Fourquet was waiting patiently, pacing up and down and holding a handkerchief in front of his face to keep his nose warm.

'Did he come out of there?'

'Yes,' grunted Maigret.

'Are you going to tell the press?'

'I'd rather this was kept out of the papers if possible. Do you have his ID papers, his wallet?'

Fourquet took them out of his pocket and handed them over.

'His home address?'

'Place des Vosges. You'll see the number on his identity card. Are you going to inform his wife?'

'It's better than letting her find out about the murder from tomorrow morning's papers.'

From the corner of Avenue de Villiers they could see the entrance to the Malesherbes Métro station and Lapointe striding back towards them.

'Thank you for your phone call, Fourquet. I apologize for leaving you outside for so long. It really is freezing cold.'

He squeezed himself into the little car and Lapointe

got in behind the wheel. He darted an inquiring glance at his chief.

'Place des Vosges.'

They said nothing for a while. In the Parc Monceau, the white powder was still falling, forming a thin layer on top of the railings with their gilded tips. After the Champs-Élysées, they drove along the Seine and soon pulled up in Place des Vosges.

The concierge, invisible in the darkness of her lodge, switched on the light and Maigret grunted as they went past:

'Madame Chabut . . .'

The concierge didn't ask any questions. The two men stopped on the first floor, where on the solid oak door was a small brass plate engraved with Oscar Chabut's name. The time was only half past ten. Maigret rang the bell. The door opened promptly and a young maid in an apron and cotton lawn cap looked at them with curiosity. She was dark-haired and pretty, and her black silk uniform emphasized her curves.

'Madame Chabut . . .'

'Who's asking?'

'Detective Chief Inspector Maigret, from the Police Judiciaire.'

'One moment.'

They could hear the radio or the television, voices in dialogue as in a play. Then the sound was switched off and, a second later, a woman in an emerald bathrobe came towards them, looking surprised.

Not yet forty, she was beautiful, extremely graceful, and she walked with an elegance that struck Maigret.

'Please follow me, gentlemen.'

She showed them into a vast drawing room where an armchair was installed in front of the television that had just been turned off.

'Do sit down, please. Don't tell me that my husband has had an accident—'

'I'm afraid that is the case, madame.'

'Is he injured?'

'It's more serious.'

'You mean . . .?'

He nodded.

'Poor Oscar!'

She didn't cry either, but merely bowed her head in sorrow.

'Was he alone in the car?'

'It wasn't a car crash. He was shot.'

'By a woman?'

'No. A man.'

'Poor Oscar,' she repeated. 'Where did it happen?'

And, since Maigret hesitated, she explained:

'Don't be afraid to tell me. I knew about everything. We haven't been lovers for a long time, or husband and wife so to speak, but two friends. He was a kind, cuddly teddy bear. People had the wrong idea about him because he'd thrust out his chest and bang his fist on the table.'

'Do you know Rue Fortuny?'

'That's where he used to take nearly all of them. I even met the charming Madame Blanche because he was keen to show me the place. You see what I mean when I say we were good friends. Who was he with?'

'A young woman, his private secretary.'

'The Grasshopper! He gave her that nickname and that's what everyone calls her.'

Lapointe looked at her intently, astounded by her poise.

'Did it happen in the establishment?'

'In the street, just as your husband was making his way back to his car.'

'Has the murderer been caught?'

'He had plenty of time to run to the top of the street and probably jumped into a Métro carriage. Since you knew about your husband's affairs, perhaps you have an idea who the killer might be?'

'Any one of them,' she murmured with a disarming smile. 'Any husband or lover. There are still people in the world who are jealous.'

'Did he receive any threatening letters?'

'I don't think so. He had intimate relations with several of our female friends, but I can't think of any whose husband would be likely to kill.

'Make no mistake, inspector. My husband wasn't a heart-breaker. Nor was he a brute, despite his appearance.

'You'd doubtless be surprised if I told you that he was shy, and that it was because of his shyness that he needed reassurance.

'And nothing reassured him as much as knowing that he could have almost any woman.'

'Have you always consented?'

'At first, he kept it from me. It took me years to discover that he was sleeping with several of my friends. Once, I caught him in the act and we had a long conversation, which ended in our being good friends.

'Do you understand now? It is still a great loss for me. We were used to each other. We were fond of each other.'

'Was he jealous of you?'

'He left me complete freedom, but he preferred not to know, with his male pride. Where is the body right now?'

'At the Forensic Institute. I'd like you to go there tomorrow morning, to identify him officially.'

'Where was he hit?'

'In the stomach and the chest.'

'Did he suffer?'

'He died almost instantaneously.'

'Was the Grasshopper with him when he was killed?'

'No. He left first.'

'He was all alone.'

'Tomorrow, I'll ask you to make a list of all the women in your circle of friends, all the mistresses you knew of.'

'Was it definitely a man who shot him?'

'According to Madame Blanche, yes.'

'Was the door still open?'

'No. She was watching through the spyhole. Thank you, Madame Chabut, and I am sorry to have been the bearer of bad news. By the way, did your husband have any family in Paris?'

'His father, old Désiré. He's seventy-three, but he's still running his bar on Quai de la Tournelle. It's called Au Petit Sancerre. He's a widower and lives with a waitress in her fifties.'

Once in the car, Maigret turned to Lapointe and asked: 'Well?'

'She's a strange woman, isn't she? Do you believe what she says?'

'Definitely.'

'She didn't show much grief.'

'It'll come. Later tonight, when she goes to bed alone. Perhaps the maid is the one who'll cry, because she's bound to have slept with him too.'

'He was a sex maniac, wasn't he?'

'Pretty much. There are men who need that for their sense of self-worth. His wife made it very clear. Quai de la Tournelle . . . I wonder if the bar's still open.'

They arrived just as a man with white hair and a coarse blue-linen apron tied around his waist was lowering the iron shutter. Through the half-open door they could see the chairs on the tables, the sawdust on the floor and a few dirty glasses on the pewter counter.

'We're closed, gentlemen.'

'We simply wish to speak to you.'

He frowned.

'Speak to me? First of all, who are you?'

'Police Judiciaire.'

'Do you want to tell me what business the Police Judiciaire has with me?'

They were now inside, and Désiré Chabut had closed the door behind them. In a corner of the room a large stove was pumping out heat.

'It's not about you but about your son.'

He looked at them warily, with the calm, cunning gaze of a country farmer.

'What's he done, my son?'

'He hasn't done anything. He's been involved in an accident.'

'I've always told him he drives too fast. Is he badly injured?'

'He's dead.'

The man went behind the bar and, without saying a word, poured himself a small glass of *marc*, which he downed in one.

'Do you want some?' he asked.

Maigret nodded. Lapointe, who hated *marc*, said no.

'Where did it happen?'

'It wasn't a traffic accident. Your son was shot with an automatic pistol.'

'Who by?'

'That's what I'm trying to find out.'

The old man didn't cry either. His lined face remained inscrutable, his eyes hard.

'Have you seen my daughter-in-law?'

'Yes.'

'What does she say?'

'She doesn't know anything either.'

'I've been here for more than fifty years. Come with me.'

He showed them into a kitchen and turned on the light.

'Look.'

He pointed to the picture of a little boy of seven or eight holding a hoop, then to the same child dressed for his first communion.

'That's him. He was born here, on the mezzanine. He went to the local school then to the lycée, where he failed his baccalaureate twice. He got a job as a door-to-door wine salesman. Then he became the right-hand man of a wine merchant in Mâcon who had a subsidiary in Paris. He hasn't always had an easy life, believe me. He worked hard. And when he got married, he was only earning just enough to keep the two of them.'

'Did he love his wife?'

'Of course he loved her. She was a typist for his boss. At first, they lived in a little apartment in Rue Saint-Antoine. They don't have any children. Oscar eventually set up on his own, ignoring my advice. I was convinced he'd regret it, but, on the contrary, he prospered in everything he did. Have you seen his barges on the Seine, with "Vin des Moines" in big letters?

'You see, to be that successful, you have to be tough. Unfortunately, because of that, smaller merchants ended up going bankrupt. It wasn't his fault, naturally. But they still resented him, it's only human.'

'You mean the murder could have been committed by an aggrieved competitor?'

'That's the most likely, isn't it?'

Désiré didn't mention his son's mistresses, the possibility of a jealous husband or lover. Was he aware of them?

'Do you know people who bear him a grudge?'

'I don't know them, but there are some. You'll probably find those who can tell you more at the Bercy warehouses. There, my son was seen as someone who had no hesitation on treading on others' toes.'

'Did he come and see you often?'

'Almost never. After he set up in business, we didn't get along very well.'

'Because you thought him hard-hearted?'

'That, and the rest. It doesn't matter.'

And suddenly, with a slightly trembling forefinger, he crushed a tear, a solitary tear, on his cheek.

'When can I see him?'

'Tomorrow, if you wish, at the Forensic Institute.'

'It's a bit further down, on the other side of the river, isn't it?'

He refilled the two glasses, drained his, staring ahead of him. Maigret drank up too and, a few minutes later, they were back in the car.

'My place, if you don't mind. You can keep the car tonight and drive yourself home.'

It was almost midnight when he set foot on the stairs. He saw the door of their apartment open a fraction and his wife waiting for him on the landing. He'd called her at eight o'clock to say he'd be back late because he'd been expecting to spend longer with young Stiernet.

'You haven't caught a chill, have you?'

'I barely poked my nose outside. Only to get in and out of the car.'

'You sound as though you've got a cold.'

'But I'm not coughing and my nose isn't running.'

'Wait till tomorrow morning. I'd better make you a nice hot grog and give you two aspirins. Did the boy confess?'

All she knew was that Stiernet had knocked his grandmother unconscious.

'Without any trouble. He didn't deny it for a second.'

'Did he want money?'

'He's unemployed. He'd just been thrown out of his lodgings because he hadn't paid the rent for two months.'

'Is he a monster?'

'No. He has the mental age of a ten-year-old. He doesn't realize what's happened to him or what lies in store. He answers the questions as best he can, concentrating hard, as if he were at school.'

'Do you think he's not really responsible for his actions?'

'That's for the court to decide, not me, I'm glad to say.'

'Is there a chance he'll be given a good lawyer?'

'It will be a young one, not known in the criminal court, as always. He's got three francs left in his pocket. It wasn't his case that was delaying me, but an important man who was shot dead just as he was coming out of the most exclusive brothel in Paris.'

'Just a minute. I can hear the water boiling and I'm going to make your grog.'

Meanwhile he undressed and put on his pyjamas, in two minds over filling one last pipe, although of course he ended up doing so. And the tobacco somehow left the unpleasant taste of a cold in his mouth.

## 2.

When Madame Maigret came in and touched his shoulder, a cup of coffee in her hand, he was tempted to say he didn't feel well and needed to stay warmly tucked up in bed, as he used to do when he was a child,

His head hurt, especially his sinuses, and his forehead felt clammy. The windowpanes were a milky white, as if they were made of frosted glass.

He took a sip and eventually got out of bed, grumbling, and went to have a look outside: the first passers-by were hastening towards the Métro station, their hands thrust deep in their pockets, mere silhouettes in the fog.

He roused himself slowly, drank the rest of his coffee and lingered under the shower. Then, while he was shaving, he started thinking about Chabut, who intrigued him.

Who had given the most accurate portrait of him? For Madame Blanche, he was simply a client, one of her best clients, who never failed to order champagne on each of his visits. He needed to spend lavishly to flaunt his wealth. He was probably fond of repeating:

'I started out as a door-to-door salesman and my father still runs a bar on Quai de la Tournelle. He barely knows how to read and write.'

What exactly did the Grasshopper think of him? She hadn't cried, but Maigret had the impression that she had some feelings for Chabut. She knew she wasn't the only woman to go with him to the discreet private residence in Rue Fortuny, but she didn't appear to be jealous.

The wine merchant's wife was even less so. Images he'd registered subconsciously came back to him. For example, the life-sized oil painting that occupied pride of place in the drawing room at Place des Vosges. It was a meticulous portrait of Chabut that was a very good likeness. Chabut was looking straight ahead of him, defiantly, and his fist was closed as if he were about to punch someone.

'How are you feeling?'

'After my second cup of coffee, I'll be absolutely fine.'

'Take an aspirin anyway and don't stay outdoors any longer than you have to. I'm going to call a taxi.'

When he reached Quai des Orfèvres, the wine merchant was still in his thoughts, an indistinct presence he was trying to bring to life. He was certain that once he knew him better, he would have no trouble identifying his killer.

The fog was just as dense and Maigret had to switch on the lights. He sifted through his post, signed a few administrative documents and, at nine o'clock, made his way to the commissioner's office for the morning briefing.

When it was his turn, he summed up the Théo Stiernet case.

'Do you think he's simple-minded?'

'That's probably what his defence lawyer will argue, unless they go for the unhappy childhood scenario. Except that he struck his victim some fifteen times and the prosecution will call it savagery, especially since she was his grandmother. He has no idea what fate awaits him. He answers the questions to the best of his ability and doesn't seem to think that what he's done is out of the ordinary.'

'What about the Rue Fortuny case, which was mentioned in this morning's papers?'

'There'll be more about it. The victim is well known, a man of means. There are posters advertising Vin des Moines in the corridors of the Métro.'

'A crime of passion?'

'I don't know yet. He did his utmost to make bitter enemies of everyone around him and there's no reason to follow one line of investigation rather than another.'

'Is it true he was coming out of a brothel?'

'Did you read that in the newspaper?'

'No. But I know Rue Fortuny and I immediately made the connection.'

When Maigret went back into his office, he was still mulling over the previous day's events. Jeanne Chabut intrigued him too. She hadn't cried either, even though she'd had a shock. She must be five or six years younger than her husband.

Where had she acquired her elegance, the ease she exuded with her every movement, her every word?

Chabut had met her during his lean days, when she was a simple typist.

Although Oscar was dressed by the finest tailors, he still remained a sort of brute, and there was still something awkward about him.

He couldn't get over having become so successful, and he felt the need to flaunt his affluence.

She was definitely the one who had furnished the apartment, though, apart from the somewhat ridiculous portrait. Modern and traditional styles blended harmoniously, creating a pleasing unity. At this hour, she must be getting ready to go to the Forensic Institute, where an autopsy had most likely already been carried out. She wouldn't bat an eyelid. She'd be able to cope with the depressing atmosphere of what used to be called the morgue.

'Are you there, Lapointe?'

'Yes, chief.'

'We're going out.'

He slipped on his heavy overcoat, wound his scarf around his neck, put on his hat and lit a pipe before leaving his office. In the courtyard, as they were getting into one of the cars, Lapointe asked:

'Where are we going?'

'Quai de Charenton.'

They drove along Quai de Bercy, with its warehouses rising up behind the railings. Each one bore the name of a major wine merchant, and three of the largest were those of Vin des Moines.

Further along, at the bottom of the street, was a sort of port where dozens of barrels stood in rows and more were being unloaded from a barge. All Vin des Moines. All Oscar Chabut's.

The building on the opposite side of the road was old, surrounded by a vast yard cluttered with more barrels. At the far end, lorries were being loaded with crates of bottles and a man with a droopy moustache wearing a blue apron appeared to be in charge of operations.

'Shall I come with you? I'll park the car in the yard.'

'Please.'

Even outside there was a strong smell of wine. After reading an enamel plate saying 'Come straight in', they found themselves in a wide, tiled corridor which also reeked of wine.

A door was open to the left, and in a gloomy room a young woman with a slight squint was sitting at a telephone switchboard.

'Can I help you?'

'Is Monsieur Chabut's private secretary here?'

She looked at them suspiciously.

'Do you want to speak to her in person?'

'Yes.'

'Do you know her?'

'Yes.'

'Do you know what's happened?'

'Yes. Tell her Detective Chief Inspector Maigret is here.'

She studied him at length, then switched her gaze to young Lapointe, who interested her more.

'Hello! Anne-Marie? There's a certain Detective Chief Inspector Maigret and someone whose name I don't know who'd like to see you. Yes. Right. I'll send them up.'

The staircase was dusty and the paint on the walls was none too fresh. A young man passed them on the stairs, a bundle of papers in his hands. They found the Grasshopper on the landing, standing by a half-open door, and she showed them into an office that was vast but without the smallest luxury.

It looked as if it had been fitted out fifty years earlier, and was dark. Here too was the pervasive smell of wine, as in the yard and throughout the building.

'Have you seen her?'

'Who?'

'His wife.'

'Yes. Do you know her well?'

'When he had flu, I would sometimes go and work at Place des Vosges. She's a beautiful woman, isn't she? She's very clever. He had no hesitation in asking for her advice on some matters.'

'I wasn't expecting to find such an old-fashioned decor here.'

'There are other premises in Avenue de l'Opéra. They're very different, with a neon sign across the entire façade, and they're modern, stylish, brightly lit and comfortable. They're the offices that liaise with the fifteen thousand sales outlets and set up new ones every month. They have computers and nearly everything is done electronically.'

'What about here?'

'This is the original place. There's still the atmosphere of the past here, and that reassures the customers from the provinces. Chabut used to go to Avenue de l'Opéra every day, but he much preferred working here.'

'Did you go there with him?'

'Sometimes. Not often. There was another secretary.'

'Who, apart from him, managed the business?'

'Actually managing, nobody. He didn't trust anyone. At this site, there's Monsieur Leprêtre, the head cellarman, who's in charge of production. There's also a book-keeper, Monsieur Riolle, who's only been with the company for a few months. In the office opposite are three typists.'

'Is that all?'

'You saw the telephonist. And lastly there's me. It's hard to explain. We form a sort of management team, but the bulk of the work is carried out at Avenue de l'Opéra.'

'How long did he spend there each day?'

'An hour? Sometimes two.'

The desk was a cylinder desk, as in the good old days, and was covered in paperwork.

'Are the other typists as young as you?'

'Do you want to see them?'

'Later.'

'There's one who's a lot older, Mademoiselle Berthe. She's thirty-two and is the eldest. The youngest is twenty-one.'

'How come he chose you to be his private secretary?'

'He was looking for a beginner. I read the ad and applied. That was over a year ago. I wasn't yet eighteen. He found me amusing and asked me if I had a suitor or a lover.'

'Did you?'

'No. I was fresh out of secretarial college.'

'After how many days did he start wooing you?'

'He didn't woo me. The very next day, he called me in, on the pretext of showing me some documents, and he caressed me.

' "I have to appraise," he whispered.'

'What next?'

'A week later, he took me to Rue Fortuny.'

'Weren't the others jealous?'

'They've all been through it, you know.'

'Here?'

'Here or elsewhere. It's hard to explain. He did it so naturally that you couldn't hold it against him. I know of only one girl who arrived after me and who walked out on her third day, slamming the door.'

'Who knew that Wednesday was your day?'

'Everyone, I think. I'd go downstairs at the same time

as him and get into his car. He didn't make a secret of it. Quite the opposite.'

'Who worked in this office before you?'

'Madame Chazeau. Now she's across the corridor. She's twenty-six and is divorced.'

'Is she an attractive woman?'

'Yes. She has a beautiful body. You couldn't call her the Grasshopper.'

'Does she not resent you?'

'At first, she'd look at me with a strange smile. I suppose she was expecting that he'd soon tire of me.'

'Did she continue to have relations with him?'

'I presume so, because she sometimes stayed after hours. We knew what that meant.'

'Did she ever appear to be bitter?'

'Not in front of me. I told you, it was more as if she was making fun of me. A lot of people don't take me seriously. Even my mother, who still treats me like a little girl.'

'Might she have wanted to take her revenge?'

'It's not her style. She saw other men. She went out several nights a week and, the next day, she found it hard to do any work.'

'And the third girl?'

'Aline, the youngest apart from me. She's twenty-two and has very dark hair, a bit fanciful, a bit of a drama queen. This morning, she fainted – or pretended to – and then she started crying and whining.'

'Was she here before you?'

'Yes. She worked in a department store before seeing the ad. They were all hired following an ad . . .'

'None was passionate enough to have shot him?'

Madame Blanche, looking through her spyhole, claimed she'd glimpsed the shape of a man between two cars. But could that not have been a woman? Perhaps a woman in trousers? It had been dark.

'She's not the type,' replied the Grasshopper.

'His wife neither?'

'She's not jealous. She has the lifestyle she enjoys. For her, he was a pleasant companion.'

'Was he pleasant?'

She seemed to be thinking about it.

'When you got to know him, yes. At first, people found him arrogant, aggressive. He acted the big boss. With women, he took his success for granted. When you knew him better, you realized that he was perhaps more naive than he seemed. More vulnerable too.

' "What do you think of me?" he'd often ask, after making love.

' "What should I think?"

' "Do you love me? Admit you don't."

' "It depends what you mean. I feel good with you, if that's what you want to know."

' "If I were to tire of you, what would happen?"

' "I don't know. I'd have to get used to it."

' "What about the other girls, opposite, what do they say?"

' "Nothing. You know them better than I do." '

'And what about the men?' asked Maigret.

'The ones who work here? First of all, there's Monsieur Leprêtre, who I told you about. Before, he used to work for himself. But he wasn't a good enough businessman to succeed. Now he's nearly sixty. He doesn't say much. He knows his job admirably and he works quietly.'

'Married?'

'Yes. So are two of his children. He lives in a house right at the end of the wharf, in Charenton, and he cycles here.'

Outside, the fog was turning slightly rosy, hinting at the presence of the sun beyond, and wisps of steam were rising from the Seine. Lapointe made jottings in a notepad on his knee.

'When his business took a downturn, was Vin des Moines already in existence?'

'I think so.'

'How did he behave towards Chabut?'

'He was always respectful, but he kept very much to himself.'

'Did they ever argue?'

'Never in front of me, and, since I was nearly always there . . .'

'If I understand correctly, he's a taciturn man?'

'Taciturn and sad. I don't think I've ever seen him laugh, and his droopy moustache made him look even more hangdog.'

'Who else works here?'

'The book-keeper, Jacques Riolle. Or rather he's the cashier. He has his office downstairs. He only deals with certain bills, what we call petty cash. It would be too complicated to explain the inner workings of the business. The real invoicing is done at Avenue de l'Opéra, and so is the correspondence with the warehouses. Here, we deal mainly with purchasing and relations with the wine producers who regularly come up from the South.'

'Riolle isn't in love with any of you?'

'If he is, he doesn't show it. You'll see for yourself. He's around forty and a confirmed bachelor, and he smells rancid. He's shy, jittery, and he has all sorts of funny little habits. He lives in a boarding house in the Latin Quarter.'

'There's no one else?'

'In the offices, no. Downstairs, in the warehouses and dispatch department, there are five or six men I know by name and by sight, but with whom I have no real contact. You probably think that we're strange people, don't you? If you'd known the boss, you'd find it completely natural.'

'Are you going to miss him?'

'Yes. I won't hide it.'

'Did he give you presents?'

'He never gave me money. He'd sometimes give me a silk scarf he'd seen in a shop window.'

'What is going to happen now?'

'I don't know who'll run the business. There's Monsieur Louceck, at Avenue de l'Opéra, who's a sort of financial adviser. He's one of the employees who deal with the tax returns and the annual accounts. Only he doesn't know anything about wine.'

'What about Monsieur Leprêtre?'

'I told you he's got no business sense.'

'And Madame Chabut?'

'I suppose she'll inherit the lot. I don't know whether she'll take her husband's place. She might be capable of it. She's a woman who knows what she wants.'

He observed her closely, surprised at the common sense of this young woman who was not fazed by any question. There was something direct about her that made her very likeable and, watching her long, slim body gesticulate, it was hard not to smile.

'Last night I went to Quai de la Tournelle.'

'To see the old man? I'm sorry, I should have said the father.'

'How did they get along?'

'Badly, as far as I know.'

'Why?'

'I don't know. It must go back a long way. I think the father found his son too harsh, insensitive. He never accepted anything from him and I wonder whether it isn't out of defiance that he hasn't sold his business yet, despite his age.'

'Did Chabut talk about him sometimes?'

'Rarely.'

'Can you think of anything else to tell me?'

'No.'

'Do you have other lovers?'

'No. He was more than enough.'

'Will you continue to work here?'

'If they keep me on.'

'Where is Monsieur Leprêtre's office?'

'On the ground floor. The windows overlook the backyard.'

'I'm going to have a chat with your colleagues.'

Here too the lights were on and two girls were typing, while the third, who appeared to be the oldest, was sorting out the post.

'Don't let me disturb you. I'm the inspector in charge of the investigation and I'm sure I'll have the opportunity to see you all individually. What I'd like to ask right now is whether any of you have any suspicions.'

They exchanged glances and Mademoiselle Berthe, the plump one who was in her thirties, blushed slightly.

'Do you have an idea?' he asked her.

'No. I don't know anything. I was as shocked as every-one else.'

'Did you find out about the murder from the news-papers?'

'No. When I arrived here—'

'Did he have any enemies that you are aware of?'

They all looked sheepish.

'There's no point holding back. I've learned a lot about the life he led and in particular about his relations with women. The murderer could be a husband, a lover or even a jealous woman.'

No one seemed inclined to speak.

'Think about it. The tiniest detail might be important.'

He and Lapointe went downstairs. On the ground floor, Maigret pushed open the door to the book-keeper's office. He matched the Grasshopper's description.

'How long have you worked for the company?'

'Five months. Before, I was working in a leather goods shop on the Grands Boulevards.'

'Did you know about your boss's love life?'

He turned red and opened his mouth but couldn't think of anything to say.

'Among the people he met here, were there some who had reasons to hate him?'

'Why would they have hated him?'

'He was a very tough businessman, wasn't he?'

'He wasn't a softie.'

He already regretted his answer, wondering how he could have been so bold as to express an opinion.

'Do you know Madame Chabut?'

'She sometimes brought me the bills from her trades-men. Otherwise she sent them by post. She's a very nice, uncomplicated person.'

'Thank you.'

Another employee, the glum Monsieur Leprêtre with a wilting moustache. They found him in his office, which was even more outmoded and provincial than the others. Sitting at a table painted black on which there were wine samples, he watched the two men walk in with suspicion.

'I presume you know why we're here?'

He merely nodded. One side of his moustache drooped lower than the other and he was smoking a meerschaum pipe which gave off a strong smell.

'Someone had a serious motive for killing your boss. How long have you worked here?'

'Thirteen years.'

'Did you and Monsieur Chabut get along well?'

'I never complained.'

'He trusted you entirely, didn't he?'

'He trusted no one but himself.'

'All the same, he treated you like one of his close colleagues.'

Leprêtre's face expressed no emotion. He wore a strange cap on his head, and Maigret thought it must be to conceal his baldness. In any case, he made no effort to remove it.

'You have nothing to tell me?'

'No.'

'He never told you that someone was threatening him?'

'No.'

It was pointless pressing him and Maigret signalled to Lapointe to follow him.

'Thank you.'

'You're welcome.'

And Leprêtre rose to close the door behind them.

Once they were in the car, Maigret's cold, which so far had only been incubating, suddenly made its presence known and, for several minutes, he blew his nose until his face was red and his eyes were watering.

'I'm sorry,' he muttered to Lapointe. 'I've felt it coming on since this morning. Avenue de l'Opéra! We forgot to ask the number.'

They soon found it because giant letters that lit up at night announced: *VIN DES MOINES*. The building, large and imposing, housed other major businesses, including a foreign bank and a trust company.

On the second floor, they found themselves in a vast, high-ceilinged, marble-floored lobby where ultra-modern metal chairs around chrome-plated pedestal tables were mostly empty. On the walls were three posters like those in the Métro stations. They depicted a delighted-looking monk eagerly anticipating the glass of wine he's about to drink.

On the first poster, the wine was red, on the second, white, and on the third, rosé.

On the other side of a glass partition they could see a huge office where around thirty people were working, men and women, and, at the back, they glimpsed more offices. Everything was light and bright, the equipment modern, the furniture state-of-the-art.

Maigret went up to the counter and had to take his handkerchief out of his pocket just as he was about to speak to a young receptionist, who waited for him to finish blowing his nose without showing her impatience.

'Excuse me. I'd like to see Monsieur Louceck.'

'Who shall I say is asking?'

She held out a notepad on which he read: *First name and surname*. Then, on another line: *Purpose of visit*.

He simply wrote: *Detective Chief Inspector Maigret*.

She disappeared through a door facing the first window and was gone for some time. She then came out of the big office and showed them into a second, more secluded, waiting room that was just as swanky as the first.

'Monsieur Louceck will see you right away. He's on the telephone.'

And indeed, they weren't kept waiting long. Another young woman, who wore glasses, came to fetch them and showed them into a spacious, equally contemporary office.

A very short man stood up and held out his hand.

'Detective Chief Inspector Maigret?'

'Yes.'

'Stéphane Louceck. Do sit down.'

Maigret introduced his companion:

'Inspector Lapointe.'

'Please have a seat too.'

He was extremely ugly, repulsively ugly. He had a long, bulbous nose with thin bluish lines, and brown hairs protruding from his nostrils and ears. Meanwhile his eyebrows, nearly two centimetres thick, were bushy and tangled. His suit could have done with ironing and his tie must have been pre-knotted on a celluloid clip.

'I presume you've come about the murder?'

'It goes without saying.'

'I was expecting someone from the police to come sooner. I never read the morning papers because I start work early. I only learned the news when I received a telephone call from Madame Chabut.'

'I was unaware of the existence of these offices and so initially we went to Quai de Charenton. If I understand correctly, that's where Oscar Chabut mainly worked.'

'He dropped in here every day. He wanted to see everything for himself.'

His face was neutral, expressionless, and his voice itself had no inflexion.

'May I ask you whether he had any enemies that you knew of?'

'Not that I knew of.'

'He was an important man and, as he forged ahead, he must have been tough with some people.'

'I wouldn't know.'

'I also learned that he was very keen on women.'

'I did not poke my nose into his private life.'

'Where was his desk?'

'Here, facing me.'

'Did he bring his private secretary here?'

'No. There are enough secretaries here.'

Loubeck didn't bother to smile, or to express any feelings.

'Have you been with him long?'

'I worked with him before these offices existed.'

'What was your previous profession?'

'Financial adviser.'

'I presume you dealt with the tax returns?'

'Among other things.'

'Will you be the person who replaces him now?'

Maigret had to blow his nose again and he could feel perspiration beading on his forehead.

'Excuse me . . .'

'Take your time. It's hard for me to answer your question. The business isn't a limited company but was owned by Monsieur Chabut, and so, unless there is a will stating the contrary, his wife will inherit it.'

'Are you on good terms with her?'

'I barely know her.'

'Were you Oscar Chabut's right-hand man?'

'I dealt with sales and the warehouses. We have more than fifteen thousand outlets in France. Forty people work here and some twenty inspectors travel up and down the country. Other offices above these are responsible for Paris and the suburbs. That's also where they handle advertising and export sales.'

'How many women on your staff?'

'Excuse me?'

'I'm asking, how many female staff do you employ?'

'I don't know.'

'Who chose them?'

'Me.'

'Oscar Chabut didn't have a say?'

'Not here, in this particular matter.'

'Did he ever make a pass at any of them?'

'I didn't notice anything of the sort.'

'If I understand correctly, you are the key man for all the sales departments?'

He merely blinked in reply.

'So it's likely that you'll keep your job, and, further-more, that you'll take charge of Quai de Charenton?'

He didn't move a muscle but remained impassive.

'Might some members of staff have complaints about their boss?'

'I don't know.'

'I assume you would like to see the murderer arrested?'

'Obviously.'

'So far, you haven't been very helpful.'

'I'm sorry.'

'What do you think of Madame Chabut?'

'She's a very clever woman.'

'Did you get along well with her?'

'You already asked me more or less the same question. I said I barely knew her. She very rarely set foot here and I was not a visitor to Place des Vosges. I'm not the sort of man who goes to dinners and parties.'

'Did Chabut have a busy social life?'

'His wife will be able to tell you more than I can.'

'Do you know if there's a will?'

'I have no idea.'

Maigret was feeling a little dizzy and he could see that this interview would go nowhere. Louceck had made up his mind to keep quiet and he would keep quiet to the end.

Maigret stood up.

'I'd like you to send the names, addresses and ages of all the people who work here to me at Quai des Orfèvres.'

Louceck's face remained blank and he merely inclined his head slightly. He had pressed a button and a young woman opened the door, ready to show the visitors out.

Before getting back in the car, Maigret went into a bar

and drank a glass of rum. He hoped it would do him good. Lapointe just had a fruit juice.

'What do we do?'

'It's nearly midday. Too late to go to Place des Vosges. Let's head back to the office. Then we'll have a bite to eat at the Brasserie Dauphine.'

He went into a telephone booth and requested his home number on Boulevard Richard-Lenoir.

'Is that you? . . . What have you got for lunch? . . . No, I won't be back but save it for me for tonight . . . I know my voice is a bit hoarse. I haven't stopped blowing my nose for the past hour . . . See you this evening . . .'

He was in quite a grumpy mood.

'They all had some reason to want him dead. But one person carried out that wish and shot him. The others are innocent, but, innocent though they may be, it feels as if they're trying to hinder rather than help us. Except perhaps that strange Grasshopper who doesn't weigh up every one of her words and who seems to answer our questions honestly. What do you think of her?'

'She's strange, as you say. She faces up to life as it is and doesn't allow herself to be fooled.'

The pathologist's report was on Maigret's desk. It contained four pages full of technical jargon and two sketches showing the impact of the bullets. Two had hit Chabut in the abdomen, one in the chest and the fourth had entered just below the shoulder.

'No telephone calls for me?'

He turned to Lucas.

'Did you send the report to the prosecutor's office?'

He was talking about the interview with Stiernet.

'First thing this morning. I even went down to see him in the cells.'

'How is he?'

'Quiet. I'd even say serene. He doesn't mind being locked up and he's not anxious about anything.'

A little later, Maigret and Lapointe walked into the Brasserie Dauphine. There were two lawyers in their robes as well as three or four inspectors who didn't belong to Maigret's squad but who greeted him. They went through to the dining room.

'What's on the menu today?'

'This will make you happy: veal blanquette.'

'What do you think of Vin des Moines?'

The owner shrugged.

'It's no worse than the table wine that used to be sold by the litre. A blend of different wines from the South and Algerian wine. Nowadays, people prefer wine with a label and a grander-sounding name.'

'Do you have any?'

'No, of course not. Shall I serve you a little Bourgueil? It will go perfectly with the blanquette.'

The next moment, Maigret pulled his handkerchief out of his pocket.

'Here we go! As soon as I'm in a heated room, it starts again.'

'Why don't you go home to bed?'

'Do you think I'd rest? I can't stop thinking about this Chabut. It's as if he did his level best to confound us.'

'What do you think of his wife?'

'Nothing yet. Last night, I found her charming and very self-controlled, despite what had happened. Possibly a little too self-controlled. It seems as if she was protective towards her husband. The indulgent wife. We'll see her later on. Maybe she'll make me change my mind. I'm always wary of people who are too perfect.'

The blanquette was deliciously creamy, the golden yellow sauce very aromatic. They both had a pear brandy and then a coffee and, a little after two o'clock, they arrived at the apartment building in Place des Vosges.

The same maid as on the previous day opened the door and asked them to sit in the hallway while she went to inform her mistress.

When she came back, she didn't show them into the drawing room but into a little sitting room where Jeanne Chabut soon joined them.

She wore a very simple but exquisitely cut black dress unadorned with any jewellery.

'Sit down, gentlemen. I went over there this morning and I wasn't able to touch my lunch.'

'I presume they're going to bring the body here?'

'This afternoon, at five o'clock. Before that, I'm expecting a visit from the funeral director to discuss where to set up the chapel of rest. Probably in this room, because the drawing room is too big.'

The small sitting room, lit by a very high window that was almost floor-to-ceiling, was bright and cheerful like the rest of the apartment, with a slightly more feminine touch.

'Was it you who chose the furniture and the wall coverings?'

'I've always been interested in interior decoration. I'd have liked to be a designer. My father has a bookshop in

Rue Jacob. It's not far from the École des Beaux-Arts and there are a lot of antique shops in the neighbourhood.'

'How is it that you ended up a typist?'

'Because I wanted to be independent. I thought I could take evening classes, but I realized that it was impossible. Then, I met Oscar.'

'Did you become his mistress?'

'The first evening. With him, that won't surprise you.'

'Was he the one who proposed marriage?'

'Can you see me asking him? He was probably tired of living alone in a small room, in lodgings where he cooked his meals on a spirit stove. He was earning very little at that time.'

'Did you carry on working?'

'For the first two months. Then he didn't want me to. This may sound strange, but he was very jealous.'

'Was he faithful in the early days?'

'I thought he was.'

Maigret watched her and felt a little uneasy, as if he had a vague sense that something didn't quite add up. Her face was beautiful, but her features were rigid, as if she'd passed through the hands of a plastic surgeon.

Her eyes almost never blinked. They were big and light blue, and she opened them wide as if to make them look even more innocent.

He had to blow his nose and, while he did so, she remained silent.

'Excuse me.'

'I thought about the list you asked me for and I tried to draw one up.'

She went to fetch a sheet of writing paper from the

Louis XV desk. Her handwriting was large and firm, executed with confidence.

'I have only noted down the names of those whose wives probably had an affair with my husband.'

'You aren't certain?'

'For most of them, no. But from the way he spoke about them and his behaviour when we gave parties, I knew fairly quickly.'

He read the names out in an undertone.

'Henry Legendre.'

'Manufacturer. He travels back and forth between Paris and Rouen. Marie-France is his second wife and she's fifteen years younger than him.'

'Jealous?'

'I think so. But she's much smarter than he is. They have a property in Maisons-Laffitte, where they entertain every weekend.'

'Have you been there?'

'Only once, because we entertained on Sundays too, at our house in Sully-sur-Loire. In the summer, we'd go to Cannes, where we own the top two floors of a new apartment building close to Palm Beach, as well as the roof, which we've made into a garden . . .'

'Pierre Merlot,' he read.

'The stockbroker. Lucile, his wife, is a petite blonde with a pointed nose who's over forty but still acts like a little girl. That must have amused Oscar.'

'Does the husband know?'

'Definitely not. Her husband is a fanatical bridge player and whenever we threw a party, a few of them would always shut themselves up in this room to play.'

'Did your husband play?'

'Not that sort of game.'

She gave a hazy smile.

'Jean-Luc Caucasson.'

'The art publisher. He married a young model who's quite foul-mouthed and is an absolute hoot.'

'Maître Poupard. The criminal lawyer?'

'He's a member of the bar and his name is often in the newspapers. His wife is American and has a large fortune.'

'He didn't suspect anything?'

'He often appears in court cases around the country. They have a magnificent apartment on the Île Saint-Louis.'

'Xavier Thorel. Is that the minister?'

'Yes. Xavier is a delightful friend.'

'You say that as if he's a particularly good friend of yours.'

'I'm very fond of him. As for Rita, she throws herself at all men.'

'Does he know?'

'He's resigned to it. As a matter of fact, he pays her back.'

Other surnames, other first names, an architect, a doctor, Gérard Aubin, from the Aubin and Boitel Bank, a renowned couturier from Rue François-Ier.

'The list could be longer, because we know a lot of people, but I chose the ones with whom I'm almost certain Oscar had an intimate relationship.'

Abruptly, she asked:

'Have you been to see his father?'

'Yes.'

'What did he tell you?'

'I got the impression that his relationship with his son was rather cool.'

'Only since Oscar started earning a lot of money. He wanted his father to give up his bar and he offered to buy him a lovely house in Sancerre, not far from the farm where the old man was born. They didn't understand each other. Désiré thought we were trying to get rid of him.'

'What about your father?'

'He still has his bookshop, and my mother lives on the mezzanine floor. She's housebound because she has trouble walking and she has a weak heart.'

The maid knocked at the door and came in.

'It's the funeral director.'

'Tell him I'll be with him right away.'

And, turning to the two men:

'I must ask you to excuse me. I'm going to be very busy over the coming few days. However, if there are any developments or if you need to know anything, don't hesitate to call me.'

She gave them her wan, robotic smile and showed them to the door, gliding suavely across the room.

In the hallway, they met the funeral director, who recognized Maigret and greeted him respectfully.

The fog, which had mostly dispersed by midday, was gradually descending again and blotting out everything.

As for Maigret, he blew his nose again, muttering disgruntledly.

# 3.

Maigret had never been comfortable in certain circles, among the wealthy bourgeoisie, where he felt clumsy and awkward. The people on the list that Jeanne Chabut had given him, for example, nearly all belonged to the same social set, which had its rules, customs and taboos, and its own language. They met up at the theatre, in restaurants or nightclubs. On Sundays, they gathered at country houses that were all alike and, in the summer, in Cannes or Saint-Tropez.

Built like a labourer, Oscar Chabut had hauled himself up into this little world through sheer hard work and, to convince himself that he was accepted, he felt the need to sleep with most of the women.

'Where are we going, chief?'

'Rue Fortuny.'

Hunched in his seat, he glumly watched the streets and boulevards file past. The lamps were lit, and there were lights in most windows. What's more, there were fairy lights strung across the roads, gold and silver fir trees, and Christmas trees in the shop windows.

The cold and the fog did not stop shoppers from thronging the streets, going from one window display to the next and queueing in the stores. He wondered what to give Madame Maigret but couldn't think of anything. He kept having to blow his nose, and he couldn't wait to get to bed.

'When we leave there, I'll give you the list. See if you can find out where each person was last Wednesday at around nine in the evening.'

'Should I question them?'

'Only if you can't get the information any other way. Talk to the drivers and servants, for example, and you're likely to discover something.'

Poor Lapointe wasn't thrilled with the task he'd been given.

'Do you think it's one of them?'

'It could be anybody. This Oscar must have made himself obnoxious to everyone, to men, at any rate. You can wait for me in the car. I'll only be a few minutes.'

He rang the bell of the private mansion and, although he hadn't heard footsteps, the spyhole cover was soon raised a fraction. Madame Blanche let him in reluctantly.

'Now what is it you want? I'm expecting my clients any time now, and it would be preferable if the police weren't seen here.'

'Would you look at this list?'

They were in the large sitting room where only two lamps were lit. She went to fetch her glasses from the grand piano and scanned the list of names.

'What do you want of me?'

'For you to tell me whether any of your clients are among these people.'

'First of all, I've already told you that I only know their first names and that surnames are never mentioned.'

'Knowing you, you still have all the lowdown on them.'

'We are in a position of trust, like a doctor or lawyer, and I don't see why we aren't granted professional confidentiality too.'

He listened patiently, then murmured, without raising his voice:

'Answer.'

And she knew very well that with him she wouldn't have the last word.

'There are two or three.'

'Which ones?'

'Monsieur Aubin, Gérard Aubin, the banker. He's involved in Protestant high finance and takes great precautions to ensure no one knows about his visits.'

'Does he come often?'

'Two or three times a month.'

'Does he bring someone with him?'

'The lady always arrives first.'

'Always the same one?'

'Yes.'

'Has he ever run into Chabut in the passage or on the stairs?'

'I ensure that doesn't happen.'

'He might have seen him outside in the street, or have recognized his car. Has his wife ever been here?'

'With Monsieur Oscar, yes.'

'Who else do you know?'

'Marie-France Legendre, the industrialist's wife.'

'Has she come here often?'

'Four or five times.'

'Always with Chabut?'

'Yes. I don't know her husband. It is possible that he's a client but under another name. That's what some of them do. The minister, for example, Xavier Thorel. He telephones me in advance asking me to procure him a young woman, preferably a fashion or artist's model. He goes by the name of Monsieur Louis but, seeing as his photo's often in the papers, everyone recognizes him.'

'Are there some who tend to come on Wednesdays?'

'No. They don't have a specific day.'

'Was Madame Thorel one of Oscar Chabut's mistresses?'

'Rita? She's come with him and with others. She's a sexy little brunette who can't do without men. I'm not sure whether it's a matter of temperament. She desperately wants attention.'

'Thank you.'

'Have you finished with me?'

'I don't know.'

'If you have to come back, please be so kind as to phone me, so I can avoid any chance meetings that would be very damaging to me. Thank you for not mentioning me to the press.'

Maigret returned to his car. He was barely any the wiser, but, for lack of a starting point, he had to pursue all avenues.

'Now what, chief?'

'To my place.'

His forehead was hot, his eyes were stinging and his left shoulder hurt.

'Good luck, my friend. Have you got the list? Go to the office and have it Photostatted, so we don't have to ask Jeanne Chabut for it again.'

Madame Maigret was surprised to see him home early.

'You look as if you've got a cold. Is that why you're back so soon?'

His face was damp, as if covered in a mist.

'I think I might be going down with flu. This is not good timing.'

'It's a strange business, isn't it?'

Generally, she learned about the case Maigret was working on from the newspapers or the radio, as at present.

'Just a moment. I have to make a phone call.'

He rang Rue Fortuny. Madame Blanche answered in a honeyed voice initially.

'Maigret here. There's a question I forgot to ask you earlier. Would Chabut telephone before coming to your establishment?'

'Sometimes yes, other times no.'

'Did he telephone on Wednesdays?'

'No. There was no point because he came almost every Wednesday.'

'Who knew?'

'No one here.'

'Except for your maid.'

'She's a young Spanish girl who barely understands French and is incapable of remembering names—'

'But someone knew, someone knew at what time Chabut was in the habit of leaving your establishment and they waited outside, despite the cold.'

'I'm sorry, I have to go, there's someone ringing the doorbell.'

He got undressed, put on his pyjamas and dressing gown, and sat down in the living room in his leather armchair.

'Your shirt is dripping wet. You'd better take your temperature.'

She went to fetch the thermometer from the bathroom and he kept it in his mouth for five minutes.

'What is it?'

'Thirty-eight point four.'

'Why don't you go straight to bed? Would you like me to give Pardon a call?'

'If all his patients troubled him for a little dose of flu!'

He hated bothering doctors, especially since his old friend Pardon so rarely managed to finish a meal in peace.

'I'm going to turn down the bed.'

'Just a moment. Did you save me some *choucroute*?'

'You're not going to eat that now, are you?'

'Why not?'

'It's heavy. You're not well.'

'Heat it up for me anyway. And don't forget the salt pork.'

He always ended up back at square one. Someone knew that Chabut would be at Rue Fortuny that Wednesday. It was unlikely that he'd followed him. First of all, it is difficult to follow a person in Paris, especially in a car. And secondly, the wine merchant had arrived at around seven in the evening in the company of the Grasshopper.

Was it likely that the murderer had waited for nearly two hours outside, in the chill wind, without being noticed? He couldn't have come by car because, having done the deed, he'd run to the Malesherbes Métro entrance.

All this was fairly jumbled in Maigret's mind, and he had to make an effort to think.

'What will you drink?'

'Beer, of course. What else would I drink with *choucroute*?'

He thought he had more appetite than he did, and he soon pushed his plate away. It wasn't like him to go to bed at half past six in the evening, but he did so anyway. Madame Maigret brought him two aspirin.

'What else could you take? I seem to remember that the last time, three years ago, Pardon prescribed some medicine that did you a lot of good.'

'I don't recall.'

'Do you really not want me to phone him?'

'No. Draw the curtains and put out the light.'

After just ten minutes, he was sweating profusely and his thoughts were becoming hazy. Shortly afterwards, he was asleep.

The night felt long. He woke up several times, his nose blocked, struggling to breathe. He would lie for a while in a state of semi-consciousness and nearly every time, he heard – or thought he heard – his wife's voice.

Once, he found her standing by the bed. She was holding a pair of clean pyjamas.

'You need to change, you're soaked. I wonder whether I shouldn't change the sheets too.'

He did as he was told, his gaze unfocused. Then he found himself in a church that resembled Madame Blanche's lounge, only much bigger. Couples followed one another down a central aisle, like at a wedding. Someone was playing the piano, but it was organ music that could be heard.

He had a mission to accomplish, but he didn't know what it was, and Oscar Chabut was looking at him with a sardonic expression. As the couples filed past, he greeted the women, calling them by their first names.

He half-awoke again and was relieved at last to see the room bathed in greyish light and to smell the aroma of coffee coming from the kitchen.

'Are you awake?'

He was no longer sweating. He was tired, but he didn't feel unwell.

'Will you bring me my coffee?'

He had the impression that he hadn't drunk such good coffee for a long time. He took little sips, savouring each one.

'Pass me my pipe and my tobacco, would you? What's the weather like?'

'A little foggy, but a lot less than yesterday. The sun will be out soon.'

On rare occasions when he was a child, he used to pretend to be ill because he hadn't done his homework. Wasn't this a little similar? No, because he'd been running a temperature.

Before giving him his pipe, Madame Maigret held out the thermometer. He obediently slid it under his tongue.

'Thirty-six point five. Below normal.'

'Not surprising, you were sweating so much.'

He smoked his pipe and drank a second cup of coffee.

'I hope you're going to take at least one day off?'

He didn't answer straight away. He was torn. He felt good, snug in bed, especially now he no longer had a headache. Lapointe was busy establishing alibis for each of the men on the list.

It was dispiriting. The investigation was stalling. He was all the more irritated since he felt that it was his fault, that the truth was within his grasp and he just needed to think of it.

'Is there anything new in the papers?'

'They claim you have a lead.'

'That's exactly the opposite of what I told them.'

By nine o'clock, he'd drunk three large cups of coffee and the room was filled with a blue haze of pipe smoke.

'What are you doing?'

'I'm getting up.'

'Do you want to go out?'

'Yes.'

She didn't argue, knowing it would be no use.

'Do you want me to telephone your office to ask one of the inspectors to drive over and pick you up?'

'That's a good idea. Lapointe probably won't be there. Ask if Janvier's free. No, I was forgetting, he's on a case. But Lucas should be available.'

Once he was on his feet, he didn't feel as good as when he'd been lying down, and his head was swimming. His hand trembled as he was shaving and he nicked his skin.

'I hope you'll be able to come home for lunch. What good would it do you to fall seriously ill?'

She was right, but he couldn't help it. His wife knotted his thick scarf around his neck, and he went down the stairs while she gazed after him from the landing.

'Good morning, Lucas. The big chief hasn't asked for me?'

'I told him last night that you weren't feeling well.'

'Nothing new?'

'Lapointe spent the entire evening chasing up the names on the list. This morning he's still working on it. Where would you like me to drive you to?'

'Quai de Charenton.'

He already felt on familiar territory and he went straight up to the first floor, followed by Lucas for whom the place was new. He knocked at the door, pushed it open and found the Grasshopper typing away in her corner.

'It's me again. May I introduce Inspector Lucas, my oldest colleague?'

'You look tired.'

'I am. I have a few important questions to ask you, one in particular.'

He sat down in Chabut's chair, in front of the cylinder desk.

'Who knew that on Wednesday, your boss and you would be going to Rue Fortuny?'

'Here?'

'Here or elsewhere.'

'Here, everyone. Oscar was the opposite of discreet. The minute he had a new mistress, he wanted to tell the world.'

'Did you leave the office at the same time as him?'

'Yes. And we both got into his car, which is quite conspicuous.'

'Was it the same routine almost every Wednesday?'

'More or less.'

'Was Monsieur Louceck aware of it?'

'I don't know. He hardly ever came here. It was the boss who'd spend a couple of hours at Avenue de l'Opéra every day.'

'Will you let me have his schedule?'

'I can give you a rough one, because it wasn't the same every day. Generally, he left home at around nine in the morning, at the wheel of the Jaguar, leaving the driver and the Mercedes for his wife's use. First he'd stop at Quai de Bercy to check the warehouses where the wines are blended and bottled.'

'Who's in charge of that operation?'

'In principle, it's supervised by Monsieur Leprêtre, who

goes back and forth, but there's a sort of assistant manager who's from Sète, I think.'

'Does he come here too?'

'Rarely.'

'Does he know about your relationship with the boss?'

'It's possible that someone's told him.'

'Has he ever made a pass at you?'

'I don't think he's even noticed me.'

'Right. Next?'

'Monsieur Chabut would get here at around ten and go through his post. If he had one or several appointments, I'd remind him. He often met suppliers who'd come up from the South.'

'How did he behave towards you?'

'It depended. Some mornings, he was barely aware of my presence. Other times, he'd say:

' "Come here."'

'And he'd lift up my skirt. It didn't bother him that the door wasn't locked and we'd make love on a corner of the desk.'

'You were never caught?'

'A couple of times by one of the typists and once by Monsieur Leprêtre. The typists weren't surprised, because the same thing happened to them.'

'What time did he leave?'

'On days when he went home for lunch, at around mid-day. When he had lunch in town, which was quite often, at around half past twelve.'

'Where do you eat?'

'A couple of hundred metres away, by the river. There's a little restaurant where the food's not bad.'

'What about the afternoons?'

Poor old Lucas was listening to all this in amazement and looked the Grasshopper up and down, unable to comprehend her attitude.

'Almost every day, he'd drop in to Avenue de l'Opéra, where he'd stay until around four o'clock. He shared an office with Monsieur Louceck.'

'Did he have affairs there too?'

'I don't think so. It's a very different set-up with a very different atmosphere. Besides, I think he'd have been embarrassed in front of Monsieur Louceck. He's the only person he seemed to be a little afraid of. Afraid is a bit strong, but he didn't treat him like the others and I don't think he ever yelled at him.'

'At around four, did he come back here?'

'Between four and four thirty. He devoted a certain amount of time to Monsieur Leprêtre. Sometimes he'd attend the unloading of a barge. Then he'd come up, ring for one of the typists and dictate letters to her.'

'Did he not dictate any to you?'

'Rarely. Or just personal correspondence. He needed someone in his office, a person of no importance in front of whom he could think out loud. That was my role. If I hadn't done any work at all it would have made no difference to him.'

'What time did he leave then?'

'Six o'clock in general, unless he felt like staying with me or with one of the other girls for a while.'

'He never spent the evening with you?'

'Only Wednesdays, until around nine o'clock.'

'Did you always come out of Madame Blanche's after him?'

'No. Sometimes we'd leave together and he'd drop me off in Rue Caulaincourt, a hundred metres from where I live. Last Wednesday, he was in a hurry and I told him not to wait for me.'

'Keep thinking about it. Try and remember who knew about your visits to Rue Fortuny.'

After blowing his nose, he put his hat back on his head. Madame Maigret had been right: the sun had come out and was making the Seine twinkle.

'Come on, Lucas. Thank you, mademoiselle.'

Just as the car was turning into the courtyard of the Police Judiciaire, for a fleeting moment, Maigret's gaze lighted on a man standing near the parapet on the embankment of Quai des Orfèvres. At the time, Maigret attached no importance to it, especially since the man immediately started heading towards Place Dauphine, dragging his leg a little.

'Did you notice him?' he asked Lucas later.

'Who?'

'A man wearing a gabardine. He was standing opposite the gate and looking at the windows. Then, when we drew level with him, he stared at me. I'm sure he recognized me.'

'A tramp?'

'No. He was clean-shaven and decently dressed. But he can't be very warm in his gabardine.'

Now in his office, Maigret was still thinking about the stranger and he went over to look out of the window, as was his habit. The man was no longer outside, of course.

He tried to work out what had struck him so forcefully

about him and ended up wondering if it wasn't the intensity of his gaze. It was the pathetic gaze of a man faced with a serious problem or who was suffering.

Could it have been a sort of plea for Maigret's help?

He shrugged, filled a pipe and sat down at his desk. He would still, for no apparent reason, break into a sudden sweat and have to mop his face.

He had promised Madame Maigret he'd come home for lunch but had forgotten to ask her what she was cooking. He liked to know before he left, so he could look forward to it.

The telephone rang and he picked up the receiver.

'A call for you, inspector. The caller refuses to give his name or the reason for his call. Will you take it anyway?'

'I'll take it. Hello . . . !'

'Inspector Maigret?' asked a slightly muffled voice.

'Speaking.'

'I just wanted to tell you not to worry about the wine merchant. He was a filthy scoundrel.'

Maigret asked:

'Did you know him well?'

But the man on the other end of the line had already hung up. Maigret did likewise and stared pensively at the telephone. This was perhaps what he'd been expecting since Chabut's death: a starting point.

This phone call hadn't taught him anything, admittedly, other than that someone, in this case probably the murderer, was one of those people incapable of remaining completely anonymous. So they write, or they telephone. They are not necessarily mad.

He had known several similar cases and, in one of them at least, the criminal had not rested until he was caught.

His head heavy, he trawled through his post, signed reports and other paperwork that gave him almost as much work as the investigations.

At midday, he walked down to Boulevard du Palais and, after a moment's hesitation, went into the café on the corner. His mouth felt furry and he wondered what to drink. He ordered a glass of rum because he'd had one the previous day. He actually drank two, since the glass was small.

A taxi took him home where he slowly climbed the stairs. On reaching his floor, he found the door opening and his wife watching him.

'How are you?' she asked.

'Better. Except that I kept breaking out into a sudden sweat. What's for lunch?'

He removed his coat, scarf and hat and went into the living room.

'Braised calf's liver *à la bourgeoise.*'

It was one of his favourite dishes. He sat down in his armchair and glanced at the newspapers, his mind elsewhere.

Could the man who had telephoned him be the man he'd noticed earlier in the street, opposite the entrance to the Police Judiciaire?

He'd have to wait until he called again. Perhaps he would even phone him at home, because the newspapers had often mentioned his apartment on Boulevard Richard-Lenoir. Besides, nearly all the taxi-drivers knew his address.

'What are you thinking about?' asked Madame Maigret as she set the table.

'About a man I saw earlier. Our eyes met and now I think he wanted to communicate some sort of message.'

'In a look?'

'Why not? I don't know if he's the person who called me a little later to tell me that Chabut was a filthy scoundrel. Those were his words. He hung up before I could ask any questions.'

'Are you hoping he'll ring again?'

'Yes. They nearly always do. They get a thrill out of playing with fire. Unless he's a poor crackpot who knows nothing about the case except what he's read in the papers. That also happens.'

'Do you want me to turn on the television?'

They ate almost in silence because Maigret's mind was on his investigation and its cast of characters.

'Have you made enough for us to have the rest cold tomorrow as a starter?'

He loved cold calf's liver, especially served the next day. For dessert, he ate walnuts, figs and almonds. Although he'd only drunk two glasses of Bordeaux he felt less numb and he went and sat in his armchair by the window.

He closed his eyes and for a long while he remained as if suspended between sleep and wakening. He realized that he was slipping imperceptibly and it was a pleasant sensation that he didn't want to dispel.

He saw the man outside the Police Judiciaire again, with his gammy leg. Was it the left or the right? In his drowsy state, the question took on an importance that was hard for him to explain.

Madame Maigret bustled about noiselessly clearing the table, and he was only aware of her comings and goings because he sometimes felt a faint draught.

Then, nothing. He didn't even know that he was breathing through his mouth and snoring gently. When he woke with a start, surprised to find himself in his armchair, the clock showed 3.05. He looked around for his wife. Muted sounds from the kitchen told him that she was busy ironing.

'Did you sleep well?'

'Wonderfully. I could sleep all day.'

'Do you want to take your temperature?'

'If you insist.'

This time, it was thirty-seven point six.

'Do you really have to go to the office?'

'I ought to, yes.'

'Then take an aspirin before you leave.'

Obediently, he took one, then, to get rid of the taste, he poured himself a tiny glass of plum brandy, which his sister-in-law had sent from Alsace.

'I'll call you a taxi right away.'

The pale-blue sky was clear and the sun was shining, but the air was still very cold.

'Would you like me to put the heating on, chief? You sound as if you have a cold. My wife and kids have got flu. It's always one after the other. Tomorrow or the next day it will be my turn.'

'No heating, please. I keep breaking out in a sweat as it is.'

'You too? I've found myself drenched three or four times since this morning.'

The staircase seemed steeper than usual and he was

happy to sit down at his desk at last. He buzzed Lucas to come and see him.

'Nothing new?'

'No, chief.'

'No anonymous phone calls?'

'No. Lapointe has just returned to the office and I think he's waiting to speak to you.'

'Tell him to come in.'

He chose one of the pipes lined up on his desk, the lightest one, and filled it slowly.

'Have you already got all the information?'

'More or less all, yes. I was quite lucky.'

'Sit down. Pass me the list.'

'You won't understand my notes. I'd rather read them to you before I make my report. I'll start with the minister, Xavier Thorel. I didn't have to question anyone. I found out from the Thursday papers that he was representing the government at the world première of a film about the Resistance.'

'With his wife?'

'Yes, Rita was beside him, so was their eighteen-year-old son.'

'Go on.'

'I then realized that other people on the list were at the same gala, but their names hadn't been published. That applies to Doctor Rioux, who lives in Place des Vosges two doors down from the Chabuts.'

'Who told you?'

'His concierge, quite simply. The traditional sources of information are still the best. Apparently Doctor Rioux is Madame Chabut's physician.'

'Is she often ill?'

'She appears to call him quite frequently. He's a fairly stout man, with a few strands of brown hair carefully combed over his bald patch. His wife is a large, red-haired mare who was probably of no interest to Oscar Chabut.'

'That's two. Next?'

'Henry Legendre, the industrialist, was in Rouen, where he has a pied-à-terre which he goes to once or twice a week. I got that from his driver, who mistook me for a door-to-door salesman.'

'What about his wife?'

'She's been in bed for a week with flu. I couldn't find out anything about Pierre Merlot, the stockbroker, other than that he was supposed to have dined in town, as he and his wife Lucile often do. I haven't had the time to check out all the gourmet restaurants. Apparently he's a food lover.'

'And Caucasson, the art publisher?'

'At the same cinema on the Champs-Élysées as the minister.'

'Maître Poupard?'

'At a formal dinner being given by the American ambassador on Avenue Gabriel.'

'Madame Poupard?'

'She was there too. There's also a Madame Japy, Estelle Japy, widow or divorcee, who lives on Boulevard Haussmann and was one of Chabut's mistresses for a long time. To find out about her, I had to sweet-talk her maid. She stopped seeing Chabut months ago after he treated her badly. On Wednesday, she ate alone at home and spent the evening watching television.'

Maigret's telephone rang and he picked it up.

'It's someone asking for you in person. I think it's the same man as this morning.'

'I'll take it.'

There was a lengthy silence during which he could hear the caller's breathing.

'Are you there?' he eventually asked.

'Yes, I'm listening.'

'It's just to repeat once more that he was a scoundrel. Get that clear.'

'Just a moment.'

But the man had already hung up.

'Perhaps he's the murderer, or perhaps he's a prankster. If he keeps hanging up on me, I've no way of judging. No way of finding him, either. We'll have to wait until he either talks too much, or makes a mistake.'

'What did he tell you?'

'The same as this morning: that Chabut was a scoundrel.'

Scores of people must have shared that opinion, including the Chabuts' habitual dining companions. He had done his utmost to arouse antipathy, if not hatred, both as a result of his attitude towards women and the way he treated his staff.

It was as if he actively sought to annoy people. But until last Wednesday, no one had ever tried to put him in his place. Had he been slapped and refrained from broadcasting the fact? Had no jealous spouse ever punched him in the face?

His attitude was provocative and he was cocksure, permitting himself to defy fate.

And yet someone – a man, according to Madame Blanche – had eventually had enough and had waited for him outside the establishment in Rue Fortuny. That someone must have had even stronger reasons than the others to hate him because, in killing him, he had jeopardized his own freedom if not his life.

Should Maigret seek the killer among his friends? The information unearthed by Lapointe was rather disappointing. People were less and less likely to kill in revenge for a marital infidelity, especially in some social circles.

Did the murderer belong to the group based at Quai de Charenton? Or was he a member of staff at Avenue de l'Opéra?

And lastly, was he the anonymous caller who had telephoned Maigret twice to unburden himself?

'Had you finished with the list?'

'There's Philippe Borderel and his mistress. He's a theatre critic for a major daily newspaper. They were at a dress rehearsal at the Théâtre de la Michodière. And then Trouard, the architect, who was having dinner at the Brasserie Lipp with a prominent property developer.'

How many others were not on the list and had valid reasons to resent the wine merchant? They would have had to question dozens and dozens of people, men and women, one at a time, looking them in the eyes. It was unthinkable, of course, and that was why Maigret was so keen to track down his anonymous caller, who was perhaps the man he'd seen that morning close to the parapet.

'Do you know when the funeral will be?'

'No. When I left Madame Chabut, she was about to meet the funeral director. The body must have been taken to Place des Vosges yesterday, in the late afternoon. Incidentally, why don't we go over there and pay our respects?'

A little later, they were on their way to Place des Vosges. On the first floor, finding the door ajar, they went in, and were immediately engulfed by the scent of church candles and chrysanthemums.

Oscar Chabut lay in his coffin, which had not yet been sealed. An elderly woman in mourning was kneeling on a prie-dieu while a youngish couple stood facing the body, which was illuminated by the dancing flames of the candles.

Who was the lady in mourning? Was it Jeanne Chabut's mother? It was possible, probable even. As for the young couple, they looked ill-at-ease and, after making the sign of the cross, the man led his companion out of the room.

Maigret followed the rites and made the sign of a cross in the air with the sprig of boxwood dipped in holy water. Lapointe did likewise with almost comic earnestness.

Even dead, Oscar Chabut was intimidating, because he had a powerful face, with rough-hewn features that were not without a certain allure.

As the two men were leaving, Madame Chabut appeared in the passageway.

'Have you come to see me?'

'No. We came to pay our respects to your husband.'

'He could almost be alive, couldn't he? They've done a good job. You have seen him as he was in life, only sadly without his gaze.'

She automatically showed them to the front door at the other end of the entrance hall.

'I'd like to ask you a question, madame,' murmured Maigret all of a sudden.

She looked at him quizzically.

'Go ahead.'

'Do you really wish us to find your husband's murderer?'

She was caught off guard and was stupefied for a moment.

'Why would I want that man to remain at large?'

'I don't know. If we find him, there'll be a trial, a major trial, which will receive extensive press, radio and television coverage. There will also be a vast procession of witnesses. Your husband's employees will have to testify. Some of them are highly likely to tell the truth. Perhaps women friends of your husband as well.'

'I understand what you mean,' she murmured pensively, seeming to weigh up the pros and cons.

'It is evident,' she added a little later, 'that it will cause a huge scandal.'

'You haven't answered my question.'

'To be honest, I'm not bothered. I am not vengeful. The man who killed him must certainly have believed he had good reason to do so. Perhaps very good reason. What use will it be to society to put him in prison for ten years or the rest of his days?'

'Supposing you had some indication about his personality, I presume then that you would keep it to yourself?'

'Since that is not the case, I haven't thought about it yet. It would be my duty to talk, wouldn't it? In that case, I think I'd talk, but reluctantly.'

'Who is going to take over the running of your husband's business? Louceck?'

'That man scares me. He's like a reptile and I hate him looking at me.'

'But your husband appeared to have trusted him?'

'Louceck helped him make a lot of money. He's a wily man, who knows the law inside out and how to use it. At first, he only dealt with my husband's tax affairs, then, gradually, he climbed up to being second-in-command.'

'Whose idea was Vin des Moines?'

'My husband's. At that time the entire operation was at Quai de Charenton. It was Louceck who advised him to set up an office in Avenue de l'Opéra and to have more warehouses in the provinces so as to increase the number of sales outlets.'

'Did your husband consider him an honest man?'

'He needed him. And he was capable of looking after himself.'

'You haven't answered my question. Is he going to run the business?'

'He'll probably stay in post, for the time being at least, but he won't go higher.'

'Who will have the power?'

'Me.'

She said that simply, as if it were obvious.

'I've always had the makings of a businesswoman and my husband often asked my advice.'

'Will you have your office at Avenue de l'Opéra?'

'Yes, except I won't share it with Louceck, as Oscar did. It's not as though there isn't enough space.'

'And you'll visit the warehouses, cellars and offices at Quai de Charenton?'

'Why not?'

'You're not planning any changes among the staff?'

'Why would I make any changes? Because nearly all

the girls slept with my husband? In that case, I shouldn't see any of my women friends either, apart from the ones who are ancient.'

A young woman came in, slim and lively, and threw herself into the embrace of the mistress of the house, murmuring:

'My poor darling . . .'

'Excuse me, inspector.'

'Please.'

As he went down the stairs, Maigret mopped his forehead with his handkerchief, muttering:

'Strange woman.'

A few steps further down, he added:

'Either I'm very much mistaken or this case is far from over.'

Didn't Jeanne Chabut at least have the virtue of being candid?

# 4.

At around five o'clock, there was a discreet knock on the door of Maigret's office. Without waiting for a reply, old Joseph, the longest-serving clerk, came in waving a form.

*Name: Jean-Luc Caucasson.*
*Reason for visit: The Chabut case.*

'Where have you put him?'

'In the aquarium.'

That was their nickname for the waiting room, glazed on three sides, where there were always visitors.

'Let him stew for a few minutes longer, then bring him to me.'

Maigret blew his nose profusely, went and stood in front of the window for a few minutes and ended up drinking a little of the Fine Champagne cognac he always kept in the cupboard.

He still felt woozy and had the unpleasant sensation of being in a world of cotton-wool.

He was beside his desk lighting a pipe when Joseph announced:

'Monsieur Caucasson.'

The visitor did not appear intimidated by the atmosphere of Quai des Orfèvres. He stepped forwards, his hand outstretched:

'Is it Detective Chief Inspector Maigret whom I have the honour . . .?'

But Maigret merely grunted:

'Please have a seat.'

He walked around his desk and sat down in his chair.

'You publish art books, I believe?'

'That is correct. Do you know my shop in Rue Saint-André-des-Arts?'

Maigret said nothing and gazed distractedly at Caucasson. He was a handsome man, tall and slim with well-kempt thick grey hair. His suit and overcoat were grey too, and he wore a smug smile that was probably habitual. He reminded Maigret of a pedigree animal, an Afghan hound, for example.

'I'm sorry to disturb you, especially since the object of my visit is not of much help to you. I was a friend of Oscar Chabut's—'

'I know. I also know that on Wednesday, you attended the world première of a film on the Resistance. The screening only began at nine thirty, so you had plenty of time to make your way from Rue Fortuny to the Champs-Élysées.'

'Do you consider me a suspect?'

'Until proof to the contrary, everyone connected to Chabut is under suspicion. Do you know Madame Blanche?'

He hesitated for a moment, and quickly made up his mind.

'Yes. I have had occasion to go to her place.'

'With whom?'

'With Jeanne Chabut. She knew that her husband frequented the establishment. She wanted to see for herself.'

'Are you Madame Chabut's lover?'

'I was. I have every reason to believe that she has had others.'

'When was this?'

'We haven't met for around six months.'

'Did you use to go and see her at Place des Vosges?'

'Yes. Whenever her husband went on a trip to the South, which was almost every week.'

'Is that why you have come to see me?'

'No. I was simply answering your question. What I wanted to ask you was whether you had found the letters.'

Maigret watched him, frowning.

'What letters?'

'The private letters Oscar received. Not his business correspondence, of course. I presume he kept those letters at Place des Vosges or perhaps Quai de Charenton.'

'And you would like to take possession of those letters?'

'Meg . . . That's my wife . . . Meg, I was saying, has a habit of writing long letters in which she puts everything that goes through her head—'

'Is it her letters you want to retrieve?'

'She had a fairly long affair with Oscar. I caught them together and he seemed dismayed.'

'Was he in love?'

'He's never been in love in his life. She was one more conquest to add to his tally.'

'Are you jealous?'

'In the end, I got used to it.'

'Has your wife had other affairs?'

'I have to admit she has.'

'If I understand correctly, your wife was Chabut's

mistress and you were Madame Chabut's lover. Is that right?'

In Maigret's voice and attitude there was a veiled irony which the art publisher did not notice.

'Did you write letters too?'

'Three or four.'

'To Madame Chabut?'

'No. To Oscar.'

'To complain about his relationship with Meg?'

'No.'

He had reached the awkward part and was trying to appear relaxed.

'You probably aren't aware of the situation of an art publisher. Customers are few and far between and the production costs are extremely high. A publication takes several years to sell and requires considerable investment.

'Which explains why we still need sponsors.'

Maigret, more ironic than ever, asked innocently:

'Was Monsieur Chabut a sponsor?'

'He was very affluent. He made money in spades. I thought he might be able to help me and—'

'You wrote to him?'

'Yes.'

'Even though he was your wife's lover?'

'There's no connection between the two things.'

'Had you already caught them out?'

'I can't recall the exact dates, but I suppose so.'

Stunned, Maigret tamped down the ash in his pipe with his finger.

'Were you already Jeanne Chabut's lover?'

'I was sure you wouldn't understand. You always hark

back to good old middle-class morality, which doesn't apply in our circles. For us, these sexual relationships are of no consequence.'

'I understand perfectly well. In other words, you turned to Oscar Chabut solely because he was wealthy.'

'That is correct.'

'You would have just as readily approached a banker or an industrialist whom you didn't know.'

'If I found myself in a corner, yes.'

'But you weren't in a corner?'

'I wanted to publish an important work on aspects of Asian art.'

'Are there things in those letters that you regret writing?'

Caucasson was increasingly uncomfortable, but he managed to maintain a certain dignity.

'Let us say that they could be misinterpreted.'

'Shallow people, for example, people who don't belong to your world and who aren't very open-minded, might be tempted to blackmail you. Is that it?'

'More or less.'

'Were you very persistent?'

'I wrote three or four letters.'

'All on the same subject? Within quite a short space of time?'

'I was in a hurry to get the book underway. One of the top oriental art experts had already given me the text.'

'Did he pay up?'

Caucasson shook his head.

'No.'

'Were you very disappointed?'

'Yes. I wasn't expecting him to refuse. I didn't know him well enough.'

'He was a hard man, wasn't he?'

'Yes, he was hard and contemptuous.'

'Did he respond in writing?'

'He didn't take the trouble. One evening when he was throwing a cocktail party for thirty or so friends, I followed him in the hope that he'd finally give me an answer . . .'

'And did he?'

'Brutally. He turned around, in the middle of the drawing room, and said in a loud voice, for all to hear:

' "Let me tell you that I don't give a damn about Meg and even less about your knocking about with my wife. So stop asking me for money." '

Caucasson's face had been pale on arrival, but now it was flushed, and his tapering, manicured hands were trembling slightly.

'You see I'm being completely open with you. I could have kept quiet and let things take their course.'

'You mean waited until I found the letters?'

'We can't know whose hands they will fall into.'

'Had you seen him since?'

'Twice. Meg and I were still invited to Place des Vosges.'

'And you went,' muttered Maigret with feigned admiration. 'I see you practise forgiveness.'

'What else could I do? He was a brute, but he was also a force of nature. He must have humiliated others, even among our friends. He needed to feel powerful, and he didn't seek to be liked.'

'Were you counting on me to give you back those letters?'

'I'd rather know they'd been destroyed.'

'Your wife's and yours, is that right?'

'Meg's letters are likely to be a little too passionate, if not erotic, and mine, as I told you, could be misinterpreted.'

'I'll see what I can do for you.'

'Have you found them?'

Maigret didn't answer but walked over to the door to signal the end of the conversation.

'Incidentally, do you own a 6.35 automatic pistol?'

'I have an automatic in my shop. It's been in the same drawer for years, but I don't even know the calibre. I don't like guns.'

'Thank you. By the way, did you know that your friend Chabut used to visit Rue Fortuny at around the same time every Wednesday?'

'Yes, because Jeanne and I would sometimes take advantage of it.'

'That will be all for today. If I need you, I'll ask you to come in.'

Caucasson finally left, almost bumping into the door frame, and Maigret watched him make his way to the staircase. He went back inside his office and asked to put a call through to Place des Vosges. It took a while because the line was constantly engaged.

'Madame Chabut? Inspector Maigret here. I apologize for disturbing you once again, but I have to ask you a couple of questions as a result of a visit I have just received.'

'Would you kindly make it quick as I am extremely busy. The funeral is actually taking place tomorrow, in the strictest privacy.'

'Will there be a religious ceremony?'

'A simple absolution. I am only telling a few close friends and one or two of my husband's staff.'

'Monsieur Louceck?'

'I have no choice.'

'Monsieur Leprêtre?'

'Certainly, and even his private secretary, that skinny girl he called the Grasshopper. Three cars will drive us directly to Ivry Cemetery.'

'Do you know where your husband kept his private correspondence?'

There was a lengthy silence.

'Believe it or not, I never asked myself the question and I'm trying to think. He received very few letters at home because people generally wrote to him at Quai de Charenton. Are you thinking of any letters in particular?'

'Letters from men and women friends.'

'If he kept them, they must be in his personal safe.'

'Where is this safe?'

'In the drawing room, behind his portrait.'

'Do you have the key?'

'Yesterday your department sent me back the clothes he was wearing on Wednesday and his keys were in one of the pockets. I noticed a safe key, but I didn't think anything of it.'

'I don't want to take up any more of your time today, but as soon as the funeral is over—'

'You may telephone me tomorrow afternoon.'

'In the meantime, I would ask you not to destroy anything, not the tiniest scrap of paper.'

Would she not now have the curiosity to open the safe and read the famous letters?

Then he telephoned the Grasshopper.

'How are things going over there?'

'Why wouldn't they be going well?'

'I have just learned that you have been invited to the funeral.'

'It's true. By telephone. I wasn't expecting it. I rather had the impression she didn't like me.'

'Tell me, is there a safe in the Quai de Charenton building?'

'On the ground floor, yes, in the book-keeper's office.'

'Who has the key?'

'The book-keeper, of course, and Oscar too, most likely.'

'Do you know whether he kept his personal papers, letters, for example, in that safe?'

'I don't think so. When he received private letters, he either tore them into tiny pieces or stuffed them in his pockets.'

'Would you ask the book-keeper anyway and tell me the answer? I'll stay on the line.'

He took advantage to relight his pipe, which had gone out. Footsteps could be heard, a door opening and closing, and then, after a few minutes, the door and footsteps once more.

'Are you still there?'

'Yes.'

'I was right. The safe only contains business documents and a certain amount of cash. The book-keeper doesn't even know whether the boss had a key. Apparently it's Monsieur Leprêtre who has one.'

'Thank you.'

'Will you be at the funeral too?'

'I don't think so. Besides, I'm not invited.'

'Everyone has the right to go into a church.'

He hung up, his head still heavy, but his mood was less gloomy than earlier that day. In the end he went into the inspectors' office where Lapointe was busy typing his report. He used only two fingers, but he was as fast as most typists.

'I've just had a visit,' muttered Maigret. 'From the art publisher.'

'What did he want?'

'To retrieve some letters. It's inexcusable of me not to have thought of the letters Oscar Chabut received. Some of them are bound to be very revealing. That's the case with Caucasson's begging letters . . .'

'Because the wine merchant was sleeping with his wife?'

'Caucasson caught them in flagrante. Although he was having an affair with Jeanne Chabut at the same time. That's only one case. I think once we have the correspondence in our hands, we'll find others . . .'

'Where are these letters?'

'In all likelihood, in a safe that is behind the portrait of our man, in the large drawing room.'

'Has his wife read them?'

'She says she didn't think of the safe. She found the key by chance, in one of the pockets of the clothes Chabut was wearing on Wednesday.'

'Did you talk to her about them?'

'Yes. And I'm convinced she'll start reading them this evening. The funeral is tomorrow. There'll be a public absolution in the church of Saint-Paul, then only three cars will drive the family and close friends to Ivry Cemetery.'

'Are you going?'

'No.'

What would be the point? The wine merchant's murderer was not the sort of person who would draw attention to himself through his behaviour at the funeral.

'You seem a lot better, chief. You're not blowing your nose so often.'

'Don't speak too soon. We'll see how I am tomorrow morning.'

It was half past five.

'It's not worth my waiting till six o'clock. I'd be better off at home.'

'Goodnight, chief.'

'Goodnight, boys.'

And Maigret left the inspectors' office, pipe between his teeth, his shoulders hunched and his legs a little weak.

He slept heavily and if he did dream he wouldn't remember in the morning. The wind must have changed direction during the night because the weather was completely different, much less cold, with driving rain streaking the windows.

'Are you going to take your temperature?'

'No. I'm not feverish.'

He felt better. He drank his two cups of coffee, savouring them, and once again Madame Maigret telephoned for a taxi.

'Don't forget your umbrella.'

In his office, he glanced routinely at the pile of correspondence waiting for him. It was an old habit. By looking at the envelopes, he could see whether he recognized the writing of a friend or someone from whom he was expecting a message.

On one of the envelopes, the address was written in block capitals. In the top left-hand corner, the word *Private* was underlined three times.

> DETECTIVE CHIEF INSPECTOR MAIGRET
> HEAD OF THE CRIME SQUAD
> 38, QUAI DES ORFÈVRES

He opened this letter first. It contained two sheets of paper, with the letterhead cut off one of them, probably that of a brasserie or a café. The handwriting was regular, and so was the spacing, and it was obvious that the author was meticulous and attentive to detail.

*I hope that this letter will not be caught up in the wheels of police bureaucracy and that you will read it in person.*

*I am the person who telephoned you twice, but I hung up straight away for fear you would trace the number I was calling from. That is supposedly impossible with automatic dialling, but I prefer not to trust it.*

*I am surprised by the silence of the newspapers concerning Oscar Chabut's personality. Is there no one, among the people they have contacted, who will speak the truth?*

*Instead, they talk about him as an important figure, bold and tenacious, who built up one of the biggest wine businesses through sheer hard work.*

*It's an outrage! That man was a scoundrel, as I've told you and I repeat. He had no scruples in sacrificing anyone and everyone to his ambition and his delusions of grandeur. I actually wonder whether he wasn't mad in a way.*

*It is hard to believe that a man of sound mind could behave as he did. With women, he was driven by the need to sully them. He wanted to possess them all so as to demean them and feel superior to them. Furthermore, he boasted of his successes with no consideration for their reputations.*

*What about the husbands? Is it possible that they were oblivious? I think not. He dominated them too with his contempt, forcing them in a way to keep quiet.*

*He needed to humiliate everyone around him in order to feel strong and powerful. Do you understand?*

*Sometimes I speak of him in the present tense as if he were still alive, whereas he has finally received his just desserts. No one will weep over him, not even his family, not even his father who has long since fallen out with him.*

*The newspapers make no mention of all that and, if one day you arrest the man who shot him and put an end to his vile doings, it is that man who will be universally condemned.*

*I wanted to contact you. I saw you go into the apartment building in Place des Vosges with another man who must be one of your inspectors. I also saw you at Quai de Charenton, where things are not as simple as they appear. Everything connected with that man is contaminated in some way.*

*You're looking for the murderer? That is your job and I don't hold it against you. But, if there were any justice in this world, he should be congratulated.*

*I repeat: Oscar Chabut was a filthy scoundrel and a deeply perverted creature.*

*Yours faithfully, and I apologize for not signing my name.*

However, there were vague initials at the bottom of the letter.

Maigret reread it slowly, sentence by sentence. In the

course of his career, he had received hundreds of anonymous letters and he was able to recognize the ones that
were of genuine interest.

Despite the pomposity and probable exaggeration, this
one did not contain only gratuitous accusations, and the
portrait it painted of the wine merchant was not so far
removed from the man himself.

Was it the murderer writing? Was it one of Oscar
Chabut's many victims? If so, was it someone whose wife
he had taken only to drop her afterwards, as was his habit,
or a man who had suffered from his unscrupulous business tactics?

Maigret couldn't help seeing the man with a limp who
had been waiting for him opposite the entrance to the
Police Judiciaire and then made off in the direction of
Place Dauphine. His appearance was shabby. He looked
as if he'd slept in his clothes, but without being a tramp.
In Paris there were thousands of people who didn't fit
into any category. Some were on an inevitable downward
slide, and ended up sleeping rough on the banks of the
Seine, unless they committed suicide.

Others clung on, gritted their teeth, and sometimes
managed to clamber back up again, especially if someone
extended a helping hand.

In his heart, Maigret would have liked to assist that
man. He probably wasn't mad, despite his hatred for
Chabut, which had become his mission in life.

Was he the man who had killed the wine merchant? It
was possible. It was easy to imagine him lurking in the shadows, fingers curled around the ice-cold grip of a pistol.

He fired as he had promised himself he would, once,

twice, three times, four times, then limped off in the direction of the Métro.

Where did he sleep? Where had he gone after that? Had he been content to reach the Grands Boulevards or another well-lit neighbourhood and gone into a café to warm himself and celebrate his accomplishment on his own?

Chabut's murder was not improvised. The perpetrator had thought about it for a long time, hesitating, dwelling on his grievances, before making up his mind to act.

But now, his enemy was dead. Was it not a little as if the murderer had suddenly lost his sense of purpose? People spoke of the victim as a brilliant man, an outstanding businessman. No one mentioned the man who had killed him or his reasons for doing so.

So he telephoned Maigret, then he wrote. He would write again, until he unwittingly said too much and gave himself away.

Maigret made his way towards the commissioner's office, because the bell had just announced the briefing.

'No news on the Rue Fortuny case?'

'Nothing specific. All the same, I'm beginning to feel hopeful.'

'Do you think there'll be a scandal?'

Maigret frowned. He hadn't talked to his chief about Chabut's personality, and the newspapers hadn't mentioned anything either. So why was he talking about a scandal at this stage?

Because the head of the Police Judiciaire had been acquainted with the wine merchant? Or because he moved in the circles where Chabut was well known? In that case, he would be aware that a great number of people had good reason to bear Chabut a strong enough grudge to want to kill him.

'I don't have any names in mind yet,' he said, evasively.

'All the same, you were right not to say too much to the press.'

Later, he sifted through the rest of his post and had a typist come up so he could dictate some replies. His body still ached and he felt weak, but he no longer had to walk around clutching a handkerchief.

Lapointe came in just before midday.

'I hope you won't be annoyed with me. I could almost say I went in a private capacity. I was curious to see the funeral. There were no more than around twenty people in total, and only Monsieur Louceck represented the employees.'

'Did you recognize anyone else?'

'As I came out of the church, I had the impression that a man on the opposite side of the street was looking at me. I tried to catch up with him, but by the time I'd threaded my way through the heavy traffic he'd vanished.'

'Here! Read this.'

Maigret held out the anonymous letter, which made Lapointe smile more than once.

'That's like him, isn't it?'

'Note that he saw me at Place des Vosges, Quai de Charenton, and probably going into the Police Judiciaire too. This morning he must have been expecting me to attend the funeral.'

'He must have seen me with you and recognized me.'

'I want us to have a man at Place des Vosges this

afternoon. He is not to take any notice of me. I will probably pay a visit to Madame Chabut. What he needs to be on the lookout for is someone prowling around in the vicinity of the building. As far as we can judge, this man is very good at disappearing into thin air.'

'Do you want me to go there?'

'As you wish, but ideally yes, since you already know what he looks like.'

Maigret went home for lunch, ate heartily and spent only fifteen minutes dozing in his armchair. Back at the office, he called Place des Vosges and asked to speak to Jeanne Chabut. He was left holding on for quite a while.

'I apologize for disturbing you so soon after the funeral. I confess I'm eager to see this correspondence, which might give us some valuable clues.'

'Do you wish to come this afternoon?'

'Preferably.'

'I have a visit which I can't put off, at around five. If you could come right away—'

'I'll be there in a few minutes.'

Lapointe was already keeping watch near the apartment building. Maigret was driven there by Torrence, whom he then sent back to the Police Judiciaire. The black drapes with silver teardrops had been taken down from the entrance and, in the apartment, there was no trace of the chapel of rest. Only the smell of chrysanthemums lingered in the air.

She was wearing the same black dress as the previous day, but she'd added a brooch with coloured stones that made her look less severe. She was very alert, very self-controlled.

'We can go into my little sitting room, if you prefer. The large drawing room is much too empty for two people.'

'Have you opened the safe?'

'I won't deny it.'

'How did you find out the combination? I assume you didn't know it.'

'No, of course not. It immediately occurred to me that my husband must always have carried it on his person. I looked in his wallet. When I opened his driving licence, I saw a series of numbers and I tried them on the safe.'

On the Louis XV table there was a fat bundle of letters, clumsily tied together with string.

'I haven't read them all, I hasten to say. The night would probably not have been long enough. I was astonished to see all the papers he kept. I even found old love letters that I'd written before we were married.'

'I think it's best to start with the most recent correspondence, which might explain the murder.'

'Do sit down.'

He was surprised to see her put on a pair of glasses, which seemed to give her a different personality. Now he understood her wish to take things in hand. She was a very cool-headed woman, who must have a fierce will and was not one to give up easily on a task she had set herself.

'A lot of notes . . . Look! . . . Here's one signed Rita . . . I don't know which Rita that is . . .

' "*I'll be free at 3 o'clock tomorrow. The usual place? Kisses. Rita.*"

'As you can see, she's not very romantic and her writing paper is cheap and nasty, and it's perfumed.'

'Is there no date?'

'No, but this note was among the letters of the past few months.'

'You didn't find anything from Jean-Luc Caucasson?'

'Do you know about that? Did he come and see you?'

'He's very concerned about the fate of the letters.'

It was still raining and the water formed rivulets that zigzagged down the panes of the high windows. The apartment was peaceful and quiet. They sat in front of hundreds of letters and notes that summed up the entire life of a man.

'Here's one. Do you want to read it for yourself?'

'Yes, preferably.'

'You may smoke your pipe, you know. I don't mind in the slightest.'

*My dear Oscar,*

*I hesitated for a long time before writing this letter, but, when I thought of our longstanding friendship, my reluctance was dispelled. You are a brilliant businessman, whereas I don't know much about figures, which is why I find it very disagreeable to raise the subject of money.*

*The profession of art publisher it not like any other. You are always on the lookout for the book that will be a huge success. Sometimes, you have to wait for a long time and, when it does come into your hands, you find you don't have the means to publish it.*

*This is what has happened to me. At a time when business was stagnant and I hadn't published anything for over a year, I received a unique work on certain aspects of Asian art. I know that it is an important book and that it will achieve a well-deserved success. It is even highly likely that I will be able to sell the rights to the United States and to other countries, generating income, a small proportion of which would cover the costs.*

*But, in order to publish, I would need around two hundred thousand francs right away, and I don't have even a centime. As for Meg, who has her own little kitty, her entire savings amount to no more than ten thousand francs or so.*

*Can you advance me the money? I know that for you, this amount is small change. This is the first time that I have asked for money, and I find it deeply embarrassing.*

*I discussed it with Meg before making up my mind to write and she said that our friendship meant too much for you to refuse this favour.*

*Telephone me or send me a note to arrange a meeting at your home or at one of your offices. I'll sign any documents you wish.*

'Nauseating, isn't it?'

Maigret was lighting his pipe and she had just lit a cigarette.

'You noted the allusion to Meg. The second letter is shorter.'

They were both handwritten, the letters small, clear and nervous.

*My dear friend,*

*I am surprised not to have received a reply to my letter yet. It took a lot of courage for me to write to you. That I spoke to you so frankly is proof of the trust I placed in you.*

*Since then, the situation has deteriorated somewhat. I have some rather large payments that will fall due shortly, which might force me to close down.*

*Meg, who is aware of the situation, is worried sick and insisted I write to you.*

*I hope that you will prove to me that friendship isn't a hollow word.*

*I am counting on you as you can count on me.*

*Sincerely.*

'I don't know whether, like me, you can sense a veiled threat behind those words.'

'Yes,' grunted Maigret. 'It's quite obvious.'

'Now read Meg's letters.'

He picked one up at random.

*My darling,*

*It seems ages since I last saw you and yet it was only Monday of last week. It was so good lying in your arms, clasped to your chest where I feel so safe!*

*I sent you a note two days ago to arrange to meet you. I went to our usual place, but you didn't come, and Madame Blanche told me you hadn't telephoned.*

*I'm worried. I know you are very busy, that you have important matters to attend to, and I also know that I am not the only woman in your life. I am not jealous as long as you don't drop me altogether, because I need you to hug me so tight it hurts, as I need to breathe in your smell.*

*Let me have news of you very soon. I don't expect a long letter, but a day and time when we can meet.*

*Jean-Luc is very preoccupied these days. He has some book or other in mind which will be, he claims, the biggest thing he's ever done. How insipid and spineless he is compared with a man like you!*

*I kiss you all over.*

*Your Meg*

'There are a lot in the same vein, some of them overtly erotic.'

'When was the last one sent?'

'Before the holidays.'

'Where did you spend them?'

'At our apartment in Cannes. Oscar must have flown to Paris for two or three brief trips. We met up with some of our Paris friends there, but not the Caucassons. I seem to remember they have a little house somewhere in Brittany, in a village that's popular with painters.'

'Did you come across any other begging letters?'

'I haven't read all of them by any means. There's a note from Estelle Japy, an enterprising widow he had an affair with for a while.'

*Dear friend,*

*I am sending you this bill that I will have a struggle to pay. I look forward to seeing you.*

*Your Estelle*

'Is the bill enclosed in the letter?'

'I didn't find it and so I don't know how much or what

it was for. A piece of jewellery? A fur coat? She was at the church this morning, but not at the cemetery.'

'I don't suppose you would permit me to take these letters home with me, so I could spend Sunday reading them?'

'I don't like to say no to you, but it would be hard for me to part with them, even temporarily.

'Come back whenever you like, tomorrow if you wish, and I'll let you read them in peace. There's a letter from Robert Trouard, the architect, who was trying to interest my husband in a luxury-apartment construction project.'

'Did he sometimes accept this kind of proposal?'

'Never, to my knowledge.'

'Trouard's wife?'

'Of course, like the others. Only I don't think he knew about it.

'Look, this is the most effusive letter. It's six pages long, full of unbridled eroticism. Not only does this Wanda – whoever she may be – feel the need to recall every single detail of what they did the previous day, but she fantasizes wildly about what they will do when they next meet. She would appear to be Russian or Polish. Oscar must have had difficulty getting rid of her.

'Another. This one is from Marie-France, Henry Legendre's wife.'

She held out the pale-blue sheet of paper. The ink was a darker blue.

*You naughty darling,*

*I ought to hate you and that is what will happen if you don't . come this week and implore my forgiveness. I have found out some pretty things about you. I shan't say from whom, because she's another of your conquests. Doubtless you probably can't remember all of them.*

*In short, a few days ago, you were at a cocktail party and it so happened that someone talked about me. Now I know for certain that you said out loud, in front of at least five people:*

*'It's a pity she has sagging breasts.'*

*I already knew you were a boor. This proves it. But I don't have the willpower not to see you any more.*

*The ball's in your court.*

'You would find it a lot more appetizing if you knew the personalities involved, if you could see, for instance, the lovely Madame Legendre walk into a drawing room in the company of her husband, her bosom dripping with diamonds.

'Now you are going to have to leave me, because Gérard is about to arrive any moment. Gérard Aubin, the banker, that is. I need his advice and I trust him completely.

'If you'd like to come tomorrow afternoon—'

'I don't think so.'

'I understand that you wish to spend your Sunday with your family.'

She had no idea that the Maigrets would be content, as always, to spend the afternoon at a local cinema and then to go home arm-in-arm.

Outside, in the square, Maigret spotted Lapointe.

'You were right, chief. But he gave me the slip. That man is like an eel. I looked for him near the apartment building, but I didn't dare go too close. After around half an hour, I glanced at the Place des Vosges garden surrounded by railings. Because of the rain, there weren't many people about. On a bench, on the opposite side, I noticed a man I would swear I recognized. He was wearing a shabby brown hat, a raincoat and a darkish suit.

'I slipped through the gate and started walking towards him, but I hadn't taken ten steps when he got up from the bench and disappeared into Rue de Birague.

'I ran, to the surprise of two old ladies who were chatting under one umbrella. By the time I reached Rue Saint-Antoine, there was no sign of my man. I get the feeling he's following you, as if to reassure himself that you are pursuing the investigation.'

'He probably knows more than I do. If only he'd speak! Have you got a car?'

'I came by bus.'

'Let's take the bus, then.'

And Maigret thrust his hands in his pockets.

# 5.

They didn't go to the cinema as Maigret had planned the previous day. The rain was heavier, beating down on the pavement, and from ten o'clock that morning a blustery wind had been blowing. There were hardly any pedestrians on Boulevard Richard-Lenoir and only at Mass times could a few dark shapes be seen hunched under umbrellas and keeping close to the walls.

And it wasn't until around ten that Maigret decided to get dressed, which was rare. Until then, he stayed in his pyjamas and dressing gown, doing nothing in particular.

He had a temperature again, not high, thirty-seven point six, but it still made him feel weak and lethargic. Madame Maigret took advantage of it to pamper him, and each time she did something for him, he pretended to complain.

'What are you making for lunch?'

'I've got a roast with celery and mashed potato.'

Just like when he was a child. The Sunday roast. In those days, he wanted the meat well done. As the day went on, he had several whiffs of his childhood.

They were snug in the apartment, from where they could see the rain coming down. At around midday, Maigret muttered, tentatively:

'I think I'm going to have a little glass of plum brandy as an aperitif.'

She didn't protest and he opened the cupboard in the

dresser. He had the choice between plum and raspberry brandy. Both came from his sister-in-law in Alsace. The raspberry was more fragrant and it only required one tiny sip for the taste to remain in the mouth for nearly half an hour.

'Won't you have a drop?'

'No. You know very well it makes me sleepy.'

The apartment was filled with wonderful aromas, barely dulled by his cold, and he skimmed the papers that he hadn't had time to read during the week.

'It's curious how, in some circles, the usual rules no longer apply . . .'

She didn't ask what he meant. In spite of everything, in spite of himself, he was still deeply preoccupied by the Chabut case and every so often he would utter some comment in connection with it.

'When at least one hundred people all more or less want to kill an individual . . .'

So who was the short man with a limp who so swiftly melted into the crowd? And how was it that he happened to be at the places Maigret went to, almost always ahead of him?

He had a nap in his armchair. When he opened his eyes, his wife was busy sewing because she couldn't bear doing nothing with her hands.

'I slept longer than I intended.'

'It's good for you.'

'If only this flu would make up its mind . . .'

He went to switch on the television. There was a western showing and he was quite content to watch it. There was a villain, of course, and he had some things in common with Chabut. The bad guy also wanted to prove to others and to himself that he was strong and, in order to do so, he humiliated people.

When the film was over, remembering his tête-à-tête with Madame Chabut the previous day in the little sitting room at Place des Vosges, he muttered:

'Strange woman.'

'Who's going to take care of the business?'

'She is.'

'Does she know how?'

'Not really. She'll take to it quickly and I'm almost certain she'll make a go of it. I'll wager that before a year is up, she'll boot out Monsieur Louceck.'

He was reading an article about the ocean floor when a thought suddenly dawned on him. What was it the Grasshopper had said about the book-keeper? That he was a newcomer. That he'd only been there for a few months. Had his predecessor left of his own accord or had he been dismissed?

He wanted an answer right away. Fired up by this idea, he looked the young woman up in the telephone directory and found her number.

The phone rang for a long time, but no one answered. The Grasshopper and her mother must be at the cinema or visiting family. He called again at around half past seven, still with no luck.

'Do you believe that she knows something?'

'She didn't think it could be important so she didn't tell me about it. Besides, it's highly likely that it's a red herring. I am following up so many at the moment . . .'

A good Sunday, despite everything. They had a supper

of cold meat and cheese. By ten o'clock, they were both in bed.

The next morning, instead of going in to his office Maigret telephoned Lapointe and asked him to drive over and pick him up.

'Have you had a rest, chief?'

'I didn't get out of my armchair all day. I feel stiff all over. Quai de Charenton, my boy!'

The employees were all there, but there was no frenzy, almost no activity, except at the back of the yard where men wearing bags over their heads to protect them from the rain were rolling barrels.

'While you're waiting for me, go and have a little chat with the book-keeper.'

He climbed the stairs, knocked at the door and was greeted by the Grasshopper's usual open and seemingly amused smile.

'You weren't at the funeral?' he commented.

'The staff were asked not to attend.'

'By whom?'

'By Monsieur Louceck. He sent round a memo.'

'It occurred to me yesterday that something had escaped me. When you talked to me about the book-keeper, I think you told me he was new.'

'He's been here since the first of July. It's odd that you should come and talk to me about him today.'

'Why?'

'Because I thought of it yesterday at the cinema and I was going to tell you about him when you came. The previous book-keeper was Gilbert Pigou. He left the company in June – towards the end of June – I believe, and that's why I didn't think there was any point mentioning him.'

Maigret was sitting in Oscar Chabut's swivel chair and the Grasshopper sat with her long legs crossed, her miniskirt revealing more than half her thighs.

'Did he leave of his own accord?'

'No.'

'What kind of man was he?'

'He had almost no personality and he kept himself to himself. You've seen the accounts office downstairs overlooking the yard. We call it accounts, but the real accounts department is Avenue de l'Opéra. He only dealt with bits and pieces.'

'Was he married?'

'Yes. I think so. I'm even sure he was. I remember one day he phoned in to say he couldn't come to work because his wife was having emergency surgery. Acute appendicitis, if I recall correctly.

'He didn't talk willingly. He seemed afraid of people and tried to make himself as small as possible.'

'Was he a good worker?'

'His job didn't require any initiative. It was purely routine.'

'Did he make a pass at you? Or at any of the other typists?'

'He was too shy for that. He started working here more than fifteen years ago, when the business began to take off. He was a sad case.'

'Why do you say that?'

'Because I'm thinking about his last conversation with the boss. I'd have given anything not to have witnessed that scene, the most painful I've ever experienced. I can picture Oscar, at ten o'clock in the morning, when he arrived from Avenue de l'Opéra, rubbing his hands together and saying to me: "Call Pigou and tell him to come up." He already seemed to be relishing what was coming and I felt worried.

' "Sit down, Monsieur Pigou. A little more to the left so you'll be in the light. I hate talking to people I can't see clearly. How are you?"

' "Fine, thank you."

' "Your wife too?"

' "Yes."

' "Is she still working in Rue Saint-Honoré, in a gentleman's outfitters, if my memory's correct?" '

The Grasshopper paused to comment:

'He had an extraordinary memory for people and the minutest details. He'd never met Madame Pigou, but he remembered that she was a sales assistant in a gentleman's outfitters in Rue Saint-Honoré.

' "My wife isn't working any more."

' "That's a pity."

'The book-keeper looked at him not knowing what to think. And Chabut said with the utmost calm:

' "You're fired, Monsieur Pigou. You have just spent your last morning as an employee of this company. Since I have no intention of giving you a reference, you are unlikely to find work for a long time."

'He was playing cat and mouse, and I found that upsetting.

'Pigou, sitting on the edge of his seat, didn't know where to put himself or what to do with his hands, and he appeared so distraught that I expected him to start crying.

' "You see, Monsieur Pigou, when you want to become a dishonest man, it is better to be a dishonest man on a large scale and to do it with a certain flamboyance."

'The book-keeper still struggled a little, raised his hand and opened his mouth to say something.

' "Here! Take this sheet of paper. I have a copy of it. It's the list of the amounts you've stolen from me over the past three years."

' "For fifteen years—"

' "You've worked for me, that's true. And I wonder why you only began your fiddling three years ago."

'Tears rolled down Pigou's cheeks. He was very pale. He made as if to get up and Chabut ordered:

' "Sit down. I hate talking to people who are standing. In three years, as you can see from this list, you have stolen three thousand, eight hundred and forty-five francs. In small sums. Initially fifty francs at a time, almost every month. Then seventy-five. Then, once, a larger amount: five hundred francs."

' "It was Christmas."

' "So what?"

' "It was supposed to be my bonus."

' "I don't understand."

' "My wife had already stopped working. She's not in very good health."

' "Are you telling me you stole because of your wife?"

' "That's the truth. She was constantly berating me. She kept saying I had no ambition, that my employers were taking advantage of me and should have paid me more."

' "Really!"

' "She nagged me to ask for a rise."

' "And you didn't have the guts to do so."

' "There wouldn't have been any point, would there?"

' "True, it's easy to come by employees like you, a small-timer with no special expertise and no initiative."

'Pigou sat stock still, staring at the desk in front of him.

' "I told Liliane that I'd asked for a pay rise and that I'd got a fifty-franc increase."

' "Your boss hasn't been exactly generous, but still it's a start." '

The Grasshopper broke off again.

'The scene was becoming more and more agonizing, and the more defenceless the book-keeper appeared, the more the boss's eyes lit up.

' "A year ago, the rate was one hundred francs. And it was last Christmas that I was supposed to have given you a bonus of five hundred francs. In your wife's eyes, at least, you had become an indispensable member of staff, I presume?"

' "Please forgive me . . ."

' "Too late, Monsieur Pigou. As far as I'm concerned, you no longer exist. It is possible that one day Monsieur Louceck will decide to steal from me. I don't trust him any more than anyone else. Perhaps he has already begun to do so, but he's smart enough not to get found out. And he won't waste small sums to have his wife believe that he's a wonderful man. He'll steal from me on a large scale and I think I'll take my hat off to him.

' "You see, Monsieur Pigou, you are a miserable wretch, you always have been and will be all your life. A miserable wretch and a frightened rabbit. Come here, please."

'Seeing Chabut get to his feet, I almost shouted: No!

'Pigou walked towards him, one arm raised to protect his face, but Oscar was faster and his hand came down on the book-keeper's cheek.

' "That's for taking me for a fool. I could hand you over to the police, but I'm not interested in doing that. You will go through that door for the last time, gather your belongings and disappear. You are a little swine, Monsieur Pigou, and, worst of all, you are a fool." '

The Grasshopper fell silent.

'Did he leave?'

'What else could he do? He even left a pen in his drawer and he never came back to fetch it.'

'Have you heard from him at all?'

'Not during the initial months.'

'Did his wife not telephone?'

'Not until September or at the beginning of October. She came here.'

'Was it Chabut who received her?'

'She was in the office when he arrived. She wanted to know whether her husband still worked here.

' "Did he not tell you that he had lost his job in June?"

' "No. He carried on leaving the house at the same time every morning, keeping the same hours and handing over his salary at the end of every month. He said he had too much work to go away this summer: 'We'll make up for it this winter. I've always wanted to go on a winter sports holiday.' "

' "Were you surprised?"

' "You know, I paid him so little attention . . ."

'She was much prettier than I expected, with a trim little figure, and she was well dressed.

' "I hoped you would be able to give me news of my husband. He disappeared two months ago."

' "And you didn't come sooner?"

' "I told myself he'd be back one of these days."

'She was casual, her dark-brown eyes expressionless.

' "Now I'm at the end of my tether and—" '

Chabut came in, looked her up and down, then turned to his secretary.

'Who is this?'

'Madame Pigou,' she had no option but to reply.

'What does she want?'

'She thought her husband still worked here. He's gone missing.'

'Good Lord!'

'For two or three months, he handed over the equivalent of his salary to her.'

He looked her in the eye.

'And you didn't notice anything? I don't know where your husband found the money, but it couldn't have been easy. You weren't aware that he was a thief? A miserable little thief who had you believe that he'd been given a pay rise. If he's stopped coming home, it's because he's gone under.'

'What do you mean?'

'A person can keep their head above water for one or two months, but the moment comes when they go under with no hope of coming up again.'

' "Would you leave us, Anne-Marie? . . ."

'I guessed what was going to happen. I was disgusted.

I went down to the yard to get some air and, half an hour later, I saw her leave. She looked away as she walked past me, but I noticed that her lipstick was smeared over her cheek.'

Maigret said nothing. He filled a pipe and lit it. After a while, he muttered:

'May I ask you a question about something that is none of my business?'

She watched him with a certain anxiety.

'Knowing him as well as you did, why did you continue to have an intimate relationship with him?'

At first she tried to laugh off the question.

'Him or another man . . . I needed someone . . .'

Then, more seriously:

'With me, he was a different person. He felt no need to put on an act, to play the braggart. Quite the opposite, he allowed his vulnerability to show.

' "That's perhaps because you don't count, you're just a girl and you don't try to take advantage of me . . ."

'He was very afraid of dying. It's almost as if he had a premonition of what was going to happen to him.

' "One of those cowards is bound to turn against me, dammit!"

' "Why do you do everything you can to make people hate you?"

' "Because I'm incapable of making myself loved. So, people may as well hate me with a vengeance." '

She ended, less spiritedly:

'There. I have never heard from Pigou. I don't know what's become of him. It didn't even occur to me to mention him to you, thinking probably that it was already ancient history. Then yesterday, all of a sudden, at the cinema, that I remembered that slap . . .'

A little later, Maigret went downstairs, knocked on the door of the book-keeper's office and went in. Lapointe was there, in conversation with a lacklustre young man with dark, ill-fitting clothes.

'Let me introduce Monsieur Jacques Riolle, chief.'

'I've already met him.'

'Of course. I'd forgotten.'

Riolle remained on his feet, intimidated by Maigret. His office was the darkest and gloomiest in the building, and also the one where, for some strange reason, the smell of cheap wine was the strongest. On the shelves were rows of green binders, as in a provincial accounting firm. A huge old-fashioned safe stood between the two windows, and the furniture, which must have been bought second-hand, was covered in ink stains and even scratchings like school desks.

Overawed, Riolle shuffled from one foot to the other, and Maigret felt as if he was seeing in front of him Gilbert Pigou in his early days.

'Have you finished, Lapointe?'

'I was waiting for you, chief.'

They said goodbye to the young man and, a few moments later, they got into the little black car. Lapointe sighed:

'I was wondering whether you'd ever come back down. It's boring sitting there with a fellow who's as dull and miserable as he is.

'But he did end up confiding in me. He's not a book-keeper, but is taking evening classes and he hopes to obtain his diploma in two years' time. He's engaged to a girl from back home. He's from Nevers. They can't get married until he gets a rise, because he doesn't earn enough to set up home—'

'Does she still live in Nevers?'

'Yes. She lives with her parents and works in a haberdashery. He goes to see her once a month.'

Lapointe was driving automatically in the direction of Quai des Orfèvres when Maigret realized where they were heading.

'We're not going back to the office right away. First drive me to 57a, Rue Froidevaux.'

They took Boulevard Saint-Michel and turned right towards Montparnasse cemetery.

'Did young Riolle ever meet his predecessor?'

'No. He replied to an advertisement. It was Chabut himself who interviewed him.'

'And assured himself that he was a lesser being!'

'What do you mean?'

'That, with the exception of Louceck, he surrounded himself with weak, spineless people he could despise. In short, that man despised everyone, men and women, those who worked for him and the friends who visited his home. I am convinced that he slept with all those women to have the feeling of dominating them, tainting them in some way.'

'We're here, chief.'

'It might be best if you don't come up with me. I'm going to see Madame Pigou and, if there are two of us, it might look too official and frighten her. Wait for me in that little bar.'

He pushed open the door of the concierge's lodge.

'Madame Pigou, please?'

'Fourth floor on the left.'

'Is she at home?'

'I haven't seen her go out, she must be there.'

There was no lift so he had to walk up the four flights of stairs, stopping from time to time to catch his breath. The building was clean and well maintained, the staircase not too dark. On the first floor, he could hear the radio. On the second, a little boy aged four or five was sitting on a step playing with a toy car.

On the fourth floor, he knocked at the door, because he couldn't see a bell. He waited a good while and knocked again, annoyed at the idea that he might have to come back.

He pressed his ear to the door but heard no sound coming from inside. Even so, he knocked for a third time, quite hard, making the door shudder on its hinges, and, this time, footsteps could be heard, or rather a sliding sound as if the person inside was wearing slippers.

'What is it?'

'Madame Pigou, please.'

'Just a minute.'

It was more than a minute before the door finally opened. A young woman stared at him curiously, clutching a dressing gown over her chest.

'What are you selling?'

'I'm not selling anything. I simply want to talk to you. I am Detective Chief Inspector Maigret of the Police Judiciaire.'

She hesitated, and finally let him in.

'Come in. I wasn't feeling well and was having a little nap.'

On entering the sitting room, she went over and closed

the door to the bedroom where Maigret caught a glimpse of the unmade bed.

'Have a seat,' she said, indicating a chair.

The window overlooked the cemetery and the tall trees lining the paths. The 'rustic-style' furniture, as the catalogues described it, came from a department store on Boulevard Barbès.

There was a record player on a pedestal table and LPs scattered over the nearby divan, suggesting that Liliane was in the habit of lounging there and playing music. There was an ashtray full of cigarette butts.

'Is it about my husband?'

'Yes and no. Have you heard from him?'

'Still nothing. I went to his office and they told me he hasn't set foot there for six months.'

'How long is it since he left you?'

'Two months. It was the end of September, the day he was supposed to bring me his pay.'

She was perched on the arm of a chair and each time her dressing gown fell open, her candy-pink nightdress was visible. It didn't bother her. This must be what she usually wore around the house.

'How long have you been married?'

'Eight years. He happened to come into the shop where I was working to buy a tie. It took him ages to choose. He seemed overwhelmed. When I left that evening, he followed me. For four or five days, he walked behind me before plucking up the courage to speak to me.'

'Was he already living in this apartment?'

'No. He lived in furnished lodgings in the Latin Quarter. He hadn't even known me for three weeks when he asked me to marry him. I wasn't too keen. He was a nice boy, but he was no great shakes.'

'You weren't in love with him?'

She looked at him as she blew out her cigarette smoke.

'Is there any such thing? I don't really believe in it, you know.'

'One question, Madame Pigou. Does your husband have a slight limp?'

'Since he was knocked down by a car and broke his kneecap, he tends to throw out his left leg when he walks fast.'

'How long ago did he have this accident?'

'Before he met me.'

'How long have you known him?'

'Eight years. We were sort of engaged for a month, then the rest of the time we've been married.'

'Did you carry on working?'

'For three years. It couldn't go on like that. In the morning I had to make breakfast and tidy up the place. At midday we'd meet in a restaurant for lunch, and in the evening I had to do the shopping, cook dinner and do the housework. It wasn't a life.'

He looked at the narrow divan covered in records and magazines, the ashtray with cigarette butts. That must be her favourite place, and perhaps that was where she'd been sleeping when he'd had to knock on the door so insistently.

Did she have lovers? He would have sworn she did, out of idleness, out of a sort of romanticism.

She wore a sulky expression that seemed to be her natural state.

'You didn't suspect anything until your husband disappeared?'

'No. I don't know if he went to work somewhere else, but he always left home at the same time every day and came back at the same time too.'

'And he gave you the same amount at the end of each month?'

'Yes. I gave him forty francs a month for his cigarettes and minor expenses.'

'Weren't you worried when he didn't come home?'

'Not really. I don't worry easily. I telephoned his office. A man answered. I asked to speak to my husband.

' "He's not here," he said.

' "Do you know when he'll be back?"

' "I have no idea. I haven't seen him for ages . . ."

'He hung up. That was when I started to feel a little concerned and I went to the police station to ask if they'd heard of him, whether he'd been the victim of an accident, for example.'

She couldn't have been very persistent.

'Do you know where he is?' she asked.

'No. I've come to ask you that question. Have you absolutely no idea where he could be hiding?'

'Not at his father's. He's lived in Rue d'Alésia for over fifty years. Gilbert was born in that apartment. He's been in the neighbourhood almost for ever. His mother's dead. His father's retired. He was a bank clerk in a branch of the Crédit Lyonnais.'

'Did the two men get along well?'

'Until he married me. I don't think his father could stand me. Gilbert, of course, took my side, so these past few years they haven't been on speaking terms.'

'Have you informed his father of his disappearance?'

'What's the point? They only saw each other once a year anyway, on New Year's Day. We'd go there together and we were allowed a glass of port and a cracker. The apartment felt like a bachelor pad.'

'How do you explain the fact that your husband continued to bring you his pay for three months even though he'd lost his job?'

'He was probably working somewhere else.'

'Did you have any savings?'

'Debts, rather! The refrigerator hasn't been entirely paid for yet and I just managed to cancel the order for the dishwasher that was due to be delivered in September.'

'Did he own anything of value?'

'Definitely not. Even the rings he gave me are junk. You haven't told me yet why you're interested in him.'

'His boss sacked him at the end of June, after discovering that for three years he'd been dipping rather nimbly into the till.'

'Did he have a mistress?'

'No. He only took very small sums. Fifty francs a month, initially.'

'So that was his pay rise, then?'

'Exactly. You kept on at him to talk to Monsieur Chabut and, since he didn't have the nerve to do so – which wouldn't have got him anywhere, by the way – he began falsifying the accounts. He increased the amount from fifty francs to a hundred. Then, last Christmas—'

'The five-hundred-franc bonus!'

She shrugged.

'What an idiot! Now look where that's got him! I hope for his sake that he found another job.'

'I doubt it.'

'Why?'

'Because I've spotted him in the street at different times of day, during office and shop opening hours.'

'Has he done something? Do you have a reason to be looking for him?'

'Oscar Chabut was killed last Wednesday by a man who was waiting for him outside a brothel in Rue Fortuny. Did your husband own a gun?'

'A little black automatic that a friend gave him when he was still doing his military service.'

'Is it still here?'

She got up and shuffled into the bedroom where she could be heard opening and closing drawers.

'I can't see it. He probably took it with him. As far as I know, he's never used it and I wonder whether he even had any cartridges. I don't recall seeing any.'

She lit another cigarette and sat down in the armchair this time.

'Do you really think he'd have been capable of killing his boss?'

'Chabut treated him cruelly and he once slapped his face.'

'I know him. I mean, I've met him. That doesn't surprise me. He's a horrible brute.'

'Did he not tell you what had happened?'

'No. He only told me that he was glad to be rid of my husband and that I was well shot of him too.'

'Did he give you money?'

'Why are you asking me that?'

'Because that would be typical of him. I can imagine what must have happened.'

'Then you really have a vivid imagination.'

'No, but I know how he behaved with women.'

'Do you mean he treated them all in the same way?'

'Yes. Did he ask to see you again?'

'He took my phone number.'

'But he never called you?'

'No.'

'You haven't answered my question about money.'

'He gave me a one-thousand-franc note.'

'And how have you managed since?'

'I get by as best I can. I answer classified ads, but so far with no luck.'

Maigret stood up, his body stiff, his forehead beaded with sweat.

'Thank you for talking to me.'

'Tell me, since you say you've seen him several times, you are going to be able to find him, aren't you?'

'As long as he crosses my path again and doesn't melt into the crowd as he's done until now.'

'How does he look?'

'Tired and like someone who hasn't slept in a bed. Does he have any friends in Paris?'

'I've never met any. We only used to socialize with one of my friends, Nadine, who lives with a musician. They'd sometimes come and spend the evening here. We'd buy a couple of bottles of wine and he'd play us his electric guitar.'

She must have slept with the musician too, and probably plenty of others.

'Goodbye, madame.'

'Goodbye, inspector. If you get any news, please inform

me. He's still my husband. If he really has killed someone, I'd rather know. I assume that's sufficient grounds for divorce?'

'I think it is.'

Maigret wrote down the address of Pigou's father, in Rue d'Alésia, and met up with Lapointe in the little bar, where he was reading the afternoon paper.

'Well, chief?'

'A little bitch. I've rarely seen so many unsavoury characters in the course of a single investigation. Waiter, a rum!'

'Does she know anything that could give us a lead?'

'No. She's never paid him any attention. She gave up working as soon as she could and, as far as one can tell, she spends her days sprawled on a divan, playing records, chain-smoking and reading magazines. She must know about the sex lives of all the stars. When her husband disappeared, she was barely worried, and when I told her that he might have killed a man, she asked if that was sufficient grounds for divorce.'

'What do we do now?'

'Drop me off at Rue d'Alésia. I'd like to have a brief conversation with the father.'

'Her father?'

'No, his. He's a former Crédit Lyonnais clerk, now retired. He fell out with his son when the latter got married.'

The apartment in Rue d'Alésia was a little more opulent-looking and, to Maigret's great relief, there was a lift. When he rang the bell, the door opened immediately.

'Yes?'

'Monsieur Pigou?'

'That's me. How can I help you?'

'May I come in?'

'You're not selling encyclopaedias? Last week four of them came knocking at my door.'

'Detective Chief Inspector Maigret, from the Police Judiciaire.'

The apartment smelled of floor polish and there wasn't a speck of dust. Every object was in its place.

'Do sit down.'

They were in a small sitting room which looked as though it wasn't used often, and Pigou went over to draw back the curtains, which were half closed.

'I hope you're not bringing me bad news?'

'Nothing has happened to your son, as far as I know. I'd simply like to ask when you last saw him.'

'That's easy. On the 1st of January.'

And he gave a slightly bitter smile.

'I had the misfortune of warning him against that girl he'd set his heart on marrying. I could see as soon as I met her that she wasn't right for him. He got on his high horse and accused me of being a selfish old man and I don't know what else. Before, he used to come and visit me once a week. He stopped coming and I only saw him at New Year. Since then, every year on the first of January, he has come to see me with his wife, as if fulfilling an obligation.'

'Are you angry with him?'

'No. He can only see through her eyes. He can't help it.'

'Has he ever asked you for money?'

'You don't know him. He's too proud for that.'

'Not even these past few months?'

'What has happened?'

'He lost his job in June. For three months, he kept to the same routine as when he was working at Quai de Charenton and brought home the same sum of money.'

'So he found another job?'

'Don't you think that's difficult, at the age of forty-five, when a person has no specialist skills?'

'Perhaps. But he would have had to—'

'Find some money somewhere. He vanished at the end of September.'

'Has his wife not seen him?'

'No. His former boss, Oscar Chabut, was killed with four gunshots, in the middle of the street, by an unknown man.'

'And you think that—?'

'I don't know, Monsieur Pigou. I'm investigating. I came to see you in the hope of learning something.'

'I know even less than you. His wife didn't even think it useful to inform me. Do you think he's done something he regrets and is hiding?'

'That is possible. I am almost certain I caught sight of him a couple of times in the past few days. And I have every reason to believe that it is he who telephoned me twice and who sent me a note written in block capitals . . .'

'You didn't tell him—'

'Tell him what? If he was the person who shot his boss, he's playing with fire, as if he wanted to get himself arrested. That happens more frequently than you'd believe. He's homeless, without any means. He knows he'll inevitably be caught sooner or later. He's not ashamed of having fired. On the contrary, he's proud of it, because Chabut was a despicable creature.'

'I don't understand.'

'I'll keep you posted, Monsieur Pigou. For your part, should he contact you, kindly telephone me.'

'I told you: it is highly unlikely that he'd turn to me.'

'Thank you for your time.'


Lapointe asked him:

'Did he know anything?'

'Even less than the wife. I'm the one who informed him of his son's disappearance. He's a fastidious little old man who spends his time polishing his wooden floor and his furniture and tidying his apartment. I didn't see a television set or a transistor radio. Let's go to Quai des Orfèvres now. It's time to put an end to this.'

One hour later, five of Maigret's colleagues were assembled in his office.

# 6.

'Sit down, boys. You may smoke, of course.'

Maigret himself lit a pipe and looked at each man in turn, a faraway look in his eyes.

'You all know the bare bones of this case. Since I began investigating the death of Oscar Chabut as he was emerging from a building in Rue Fortuny, a man has apparently been taking an interest in my comings and goings. He is clever, because he seems to anticipate my every move. He is adept at vanishing quickly into the crowd, because I haven't managed to catch up with him yet.'

It was already dusk, but no one had turned the lights on and this meeting was taking place in semi-darkness. It was very warm in the office. They had had to bring in two chairs from the adjacent room.

'I have no proof of this individual's culpability. Only conjecture. And also his insistence on behaving like a fugitive.

'I have known his identity since this afternoon, and I also know his background, which sounds unbelievable at first.

'He is the wine merchant's book-keeper. A lowly man. A small-timer. He's been married for eight years. His wife, who was a sales assistant, very quickly stopped working and criticized him for not earning more. Make a note of her name and address, Lourtie. I'll tell you why later.

Liliane Pigou, 57a, Rue Froidevaux. It's opposite the Montparnasse cemetery. She spends most of her time sprawled half-naked on a divan, listening to records, chain-smoking and reading magazines and comics.

'I've called you in because I've decided to lay hands on him at all costs. He's probably armed, but I don't think he'll try to shoot.

'You, Janvier, pick six men to pair up and work shifts at Quai des Orfèvres. The individual has telephoned me here twice, written me quite a long letter, and spied on me from across the road at least once. Regrettably, he managed to slip away before I could catch up with him.'

The air was becoming a bluish haze. Maigret turned on the desk light with the green lampshade but not the ceiling light, so parts of the room were still in shadow, with only the faces standing out.

'All of you, make a note of his description. He is shortish, less than one metre seventy. He's not fat but on the plump side, with a very round face. He's wearing a dark-brown suit and a crumpled raincoat. He smokes cigarettes. And lastly, he walks with a limp. Since an accident he had a few years ago, he throws his left leg out to the side when he walks.'

'Dark hair?' asked Lourtie.

'Dark hair, yes, and also brown eyes, and thickish lips. He looks not exactly like a tramp but like a man who's at the end of his tether.

'The reason I want two men on duty is because of his skill at disappearing.

'Understood, Janvier?'

'Yes, chief.'

Maigret turned to chubby Lourtie, who was puffing on his pipe.

'What I just said to Janvier applies to you too. You don't need to remain on duty yourselves, but you must ensure your men are in position and relieve each other regularly.'

'We will.'

'Now you, Torrence. A team of six, like the others. We're pulling out all the stops. I don't want to risk him slipping through our fingers. Your patch is Place des Vosges, around the Chabuts' home. Madame Chabut is a beautiful woman of around forty, very elegant, dressed by the top fashion houses. She has a driver and a Mercedes. She may sometimes use her husband's car, a red Jaguar convertible.'

They looked at one another like schoolboys in the classroom.

'And now, Lucas. You, Lucas, will cover Quai de Charenton. Today is Saturday. There shouldn't be anyone in the offices or the warehouse this afternoon, and no one tomorrow either. I don't know whether there are security guards.'

'Understood, chief.'

'I'm staking out the places where he's most likely to appear. He never comes very close. He seems to be intrigued by our investigation, trying by any means possible to guess what's happening and what is going to happen.

'I wonder whether perhaps, deep down, he is secretly hoping to be caught.'

'What about me?' asked Lapointe.

'You stay here, on call, ready to come and pick me up

at any hour. You will also coordinate all the intelligence you receive and keep me updated by telephone.'

They thought the briefing was over and were about to stand up when Maigret raised his hand to stop them.

'There are still some unanswered questions. This man lost his job at the end of June. As far as we can ascertain, he had no savings, unless he hid them from his wife, to whom he gave his monthly pay packet. His boss didn't pay him for June, keeping that sum to reimburse some of the money he'd embezzled. Yet on the 30th of June he went home with the same amount as every month.

'Until September, he left his apartment every morning and came home at the same time as usual, so his wife was unaware that he no longer worked at Quai de Charenton.

'I presume he looked for work but didn't find any.

'In September, he disappeared. Since then, it would appear that he's hit rock bottom, that he's given up the struggle, and, from the look of him, he doesn't sleep in a bed at night.

'He must have found a few francs a day even if only to eat. Now, there's one place that is a magnet for people on the streets, and that is Les Halles. I don't know where they'll go when the market moves to Rungis, in a few months' time.'

The telephone rang.

'Hello! Inspector Maigret? It's the same man again. He insists on talking to you in person.'

'Put him through.'

And he said to the others:

'It's him!'

'Hello, yes. I'm listening . . .'

'You went to see my wife. I knew you would. You spent a long time with her while your inspector waited in a nearby bar. Is she very angry with me?'

'In my opinion, not at all.'

'She's not too unhappy?'

'She didn't give me the impression of someone who is unhappy.'

'Did she mention money at all?'

'No.'

'I wonder what she's living on.'

'She went to see Chabut a few weeks ago and he gave her a thousand francs.'

There was a snigger on the other end of the line.

'What did my father tell you?'

It was staggering. He knew almost everything that Maigret had done, although he didn't have a car or any money to take taxis. He criss-crossed Paris unnoticed with his limp and vanished as if by magic the moment he was recognized.

'He didn't tell me anything in particular. I gathered that he doesn't like your wife very much.'

'You mean he hates her. That's why we fell out. I had to choose between her and him . . .'

He appeared to have backed the wrong horse.

'Why don't you come and see me here at Quai des Orfèvres, so we can have a conversation face to face? If you didn't kill Chabut, you will leave as free as when you came in. If you did, a good lawyer will ensure you receive the minimum sentence, if he doesn't manage to get you acquitted. Hello . . .! Hello . . .!'

Gilbert Pigou had hung up.

'You heard. He already knows I went to see his wife in their apartment and that I paid a visit to his father.'

It was almost a game at which, so far, Pigou was winning hands down. And yet, he wasn't especially smart. On the contrary.

'Where was I? Oh, yes! Les Halles. It's the place in Paris where there's the best chance of finding someone who's sinking fast. From tonight, I want a dozen officers to go over the area with a fine-tooth comb. They can enlist the help of the inspectors of the first arrondissement, who know the neighbourhood inside-out.'

Would all these measures turn out to be useless? There was no harm in hoping, but the chances of Pigou letting himself get caught were slim. He might even be outside once again, on the pavement opposite, watching the lit windows of Maigret's office.

'That's all, boys.'

Just as they were rising to their feet like schoolboys and were about to head for the door, Maigret spoke again.

'An important order. None of the men must be armed. You neither. I don't want him to be shot at any cost, no matter what happens.'

'Supposing he shoots first,' grumbled chubby Lourtie.

'I said "at any cost". Besides, he won't shoot. I insist on having him brought in alive and well.'

It was half past five. Maigret had done everything he could. All that remained was for him to wait and let things unfold. He was tired and his flu was still hampering him.

'Lapointe. Stay for a minute. What do you think of my plan?'

'It might just work.'

Lapointe wasn't convinced.

'If you want my honest opinion, either we'll nab him by chance, heaven knows when, or he'll give us the slip for as long as he's decided not to let himself get caught.'

'I'm tempted to think so too, but I have to take action. Drive me home, would you? I can't wait to put my slippers on and sit by the fire, can't wait to be in my bed either.'

His head was throbbing and he could feel the beginnings of a sore throat. Was his flu in fact a throat infection?

When he was in the car, he gazed curiously about him but didn't spot the figure that was causing him so much concern.

'Stop off at the Brasserie Dauphine for a moment.'

He had an unpleasant taste in his mouth and felt the need for a nice cool beer before going home.

'What will you have?'

'A beer as well. It was hot in your office.'

Maigret drank two, thirstily, wiped his mouth and relit his pipe. At Châtelet, they saw the Christmas illuminations and the fairy lights strung across the street. In a department store, Christmas carols were blaring from loudspeakers.

In front of his apartment building too, he looked left and right in the hope of glimpsing Pigou, but he couldn't see any shadowy form resembling him.

'Goodnight, my boy.'

'I hope you feel better, chief.'

He climbed the stairs slowly and was breathless when he reached his landing, where Madame Maigret was waiting for him. She immediately saw that he was no better and that he was becoming downhearted.

'Come in quickly. Don't catch cold.'

On the contrary, he was too hot and was sweating. He removed his heavy overcoat and scarf, loosened his tie and sank into his armchair with a sigh.

'My throat's starting to hurt.'

She wasn't overly worried by his illness because almost every year he had a dose of flu lasting one or two weeks. He tended to forget it, and hated not feeling himself.

'Did anyone telephone?'

'Are you expecting a call?'

'More or less. He called me earlier at the office and he must know our address here. He's in a desperate state and feels compelled to make contact with me.'

This reminded him of past cases, particularly the one of a murderer who, for almost thirty days, had written him daily letters running to several pages, from a different café each time, judging by the letterhead. To catch him would have meant watching every bar and café in Paris, and there weren't sufficient police resources to do that.

One morning, in the aquarium, the glass-walled waiting room at Quai des Orfèvres, Maigret had spotted a shortish, middle-aged gentleman waiting patiently.

It was his man.

'What's for dinner?'

'Skate with black butter. That won't be too heavy for you?'

'It's not my stomach that's troubling me.'

'Do you want me to call Pardon?'

'Leave the poor man in peace. He has enough work with those who are seriously ill.'

'Why don't I bring you dinner in bed?'

'For the sheets to be soaked through within an hour?'

The only thing he agreed to do was to get undressed and put on his pyjamas and dressing gown and slippers. He tried to read the newspaper, but his mind was elsewhere. He kept thinking of Pigou, the humble book-keeper turned thief because his wife disparaged him for being afraid of his boss and not having the gumption to ask for a rise.

Where was he right now? Did he still have a little money? Where and how had he got hold of it?

He thought about Chabut too, arrogant, having nothing but contempt for others, feeling the need to make himself disagreeable. He had succeeded brazenly in business, but that hadn't made him any less vulnerable; he was the same man who had been a door-to-door salesman in the hope of securing an order for a case of wine.

Maigret had encountered other shy people who resented all those around them.

'Dinner's ready.'

He wasn't hungry, but he ate all the same. He found it hard to swallow. Maybe the next day his voice would be hoarse?

The squad from Quai des Orfèvres must already be in position at the various locations assigned to them. Maigret had almost added:

'Have a pair stationed opposite my apartment on Boulevard Richard-Lenoir.'

A sort of human respect had prevented him. Almost as if he were afraid. On leaving the table, he went over and glanced out of the window. It wasn't raining, but there was a strong wind, an easterly again, which would bring a cold chill. He saw two sweethearts walking arm-in-arm, stopping every few metres to kiss.

He also noticed police officers on bicycles, wearing hooded capes, leisurely making their rounds. Most windows on the opposite side of the street were lit and, behind some curtains, silhouettes could be seen, including those of an entire family sitting at a circular table.

'Aren't you going to watch television?'

'No.'

He didn't feel like doing anything. Only grumbling, as always when he felt out of sorts or an investigation was dragging on.

He refused to go to bed earlier than usual and went back to skimming the newspaper. Half an hour later, he went over and stood by the window again, scanning the street for a shape that had become almost familiar.

There was no one on the pavement, and only a taxi was driving down the boulevard.

'Do you think he'll come?'

'How would I know?'

'You look as though you're expecting something.'

'I'm always expecting something. It could just as easily be a telephone call from Lapointe.'

'Is he on duty?'

'All night. His job is to coordinate any intelligence that comes in.'

'Do you think the man is beginning to panic?'

'No. He's staying calm. He doesn't seem to be aware of the situation he's in. He's a man who's been humiliated all his life. For years, he bowed his head. All of a sudden, he feels liberated in a way. The entire police force is looking for him but isn't able to lay hands on him. Isn't that a sort of victory? He's become someone important.'

'And he'll be even more important when he's on trial.'

'That's why he can't make up his mind whether to let himself be caught or to carry on playing cat-and-mouse with us.'

He went back to the newspaper. His pipe didn't taste good, but he smoked it anyway, as a matter of principle, so to speak. He didn't want to give in either, give in to the flu, and he kept his eyes open even though his eyelids were red and prickling.

At half past nine, he got up again and went over to the window. There was a man standing on the opposite pavement, a man who was looking up and appeared to be staring at the windows of the Maigrets' apartment.

Madame Maigret, who was sitting by the table, opened her mouth to ask a question. At the same time her gaze fell on her husband's broad back. Maigret was standing stock still, tense, appearing more solid than ever.

There was something mysterious, almost solemn, in his sudden paralysis.

Maigret looked at the man without daring to move, as if he were afraid of scaring him, while the man gazed at him through the net curtains where all he could probably see was a silhouette.

One day, in Meung-sur-Loire, when Maigret had been lounging in a deckchair, a squirrel had come down from the plane tree at the bottom of the garden.

At first, it had kept perfectly still and he could see its heart pounding beneath the silky fur on its chest. Then it crept a few centimetres closer and froze again.

While Maigret hardly dared breathe, the little red

animal stared at him fixedly, seemingly fascinated by him, but its entire body remained taut, ready to flee.

It all unfolded as if in slow-motion, step by step. The squirrel grew bolder, reducing the distance between them by a good metre. This cautious approach had gone on for more than ten minutes and the squirrel had ended up barely fifty metres from Maigret's dangling hand.

Did it want to be stroked? In any case, that wasn't going to happen this time. It had looked at Maigret's hand, then his face, then the hand again and scampered nimbly back to the tree.

This memory came back to Maigret as he stared at the shape of the man on the pavement opposite. Gilbert Pigou too was as if entranced by Maigret, in whose footsteps he'd been following, in a way, throughout the investigation.

But, just like the squirrel, he was ready to scamper at the slightest warning. There was no point Maigret getting dressed and going downstairs. He would find the pavement deserted. Telephoning the nearest police station would be futile too.

Was the man trying to summon the courage to cross the road and enter the building? It wasn't impossible. He had no friends, no one to confide in.

He had done what he had decided to do: kill Oscar Chabut. Then he'd run away. Why run away? A reflex, most likely. What was he planning to do now? Carry on acting like a hunted man?

It must have gone on for ten minutes, as with the squirrel. At one point the man took a step forward, but, almost at once, he turned around and, after one last glance up at the window, walked off in the direction of Rue du Chemin-Vert.

Maigret's bulky form relaxed. He stayed in front of the window for a moment, as if to get back to his usual self, then he went to take a pipe from the dresser.

'Was it him?'

'Yes.'

'Do you think he wants to come and see you?'

'He's tempted. I think he's afraid of being disappointed. A man like him is very prickly. He wants to be understood, but at the same time he believes no one can understand him.'

'What is he going to do?'

'Probably walk, go heaven knows where, alone, mulling his thoughts over in his head, maybe muttering out loud.'

He had barely sat back down in his armchair when the telephone rang, and he picked up the receiver.

'Yes?'

'Inspector Maigret?'

'Yes, my boy.'

He recognized Lapointe's voice.

'We've already got a result, chief. Thanks to the squad from the first arrondissement, and especially to one of them, Inspector Lebœuf in particular, who knows Les Halles like the back of his hand. Until a fortnight ago, Pigou occupied a room, if you can call it a room, in Rue de la Grande-Truanderie.'

Maigret knew that street, which, at night, was like an eighteenth-century slum. All you saw were human wretches who had gathered to drink red wine or broth in sordid bars. Some spent the night there, sitting on their chairs or leaning against the wall. There were as many women as men and they were not the least drunk or the least filthy.

They were really the lowest of the low, the dregs, and it was more squalid there than under the bridges. In the street with its ancient cobblestones, other women, most of them elderly and shapeless, waited for clients in the doorways of lodging houses.

'He was at the Hôtel du Cygne. Three francs a day for an iron bedstead and a straw mattress. No running water. Toilets in the yard.'

'I know it.'

'It seems that at night he worked unloading the fruit and vegetable lorries. He only came back in the small hours and stayed in bed most of the day.'

'When did he leave the hotel?'

'The owner says he hasn't seen him for two weeks. His room was rented out to someone else straight away.'

'Are they still searching the neighbourhood?'

'Yes. There are fifteen of them on the case. The officers from the first arrondissement are asking whether they should organize a raid, as they sometimes do.'

'That's the last thing I want. You did tell them to keep a low profile, didn't you?'

'Yes, chief.'

'Any news from the others?'

'Nothing.'

'A few minutes ago, Pigou was here, on Boulevard Richard-Lenoir.'

'Did you see him?'

'From my window. He was standing on the pavement opposite.'

'Didn't you try to talk to him?'

'No.'

'Did he leave?'

'Yes. Perhaps he'll be back. It's possible that he'll change his mind at the last minute and walk away again.'

'Do you have any other instructions for me?'

'No. Goodnight, my boy.'

'Goodnight, chief.'

Maigret felt weighed down and, before sitting down again, he poured himself a little glass of plum brandy.

'Don't you think that will make you hot?'

'People drink grogs when they have flu, don't they? Which doesn't please Pardon, by the way.'

'It's time we invited them to dinner. We haven't seen them for over a month.'

'Let me wrap this up. Lapointe has news. We now know where Pigou spent several weeks, if not months. In a hovel in Les Halles poetically called the Hôtel du Cygne.'

'Has he left there?'

'Two weeks ago.'

Maigret refused to go to bed before a reasonable hour, and the earliest reasonable hour for him was ten o'clock. From time to time, he glanced at the clock, then he tried to read his newspaper. After scanning a few lines, he would have been incapable of saying what they were about.

'You're dropping with exhaustion.'

'In ten minutes we'll go to bed.'

'Well, take your temperature.'

'If you like.'

She brought him the thermometer and he kept it obediently under his tongue for five minutes.

'Thirty-eight.'

'Tomorrow, if you still have a fever, I'm telephoning Pardon, whether you like it or not.'

'Tomorrow's Sunday.'

'Pardon will still come out.'

Madame Maigret went to change into her nightdress. She talked to him from the bedroom.

'I don't like it when your throat starts getting red. In a minute, I'm going to dab it.'

'You know that's likely to make me vomit.'

'You won't feel a thing. You said the same thing last time and everything was fine.'

She'd painted a viscous liquid based on methylene blue on his throat with a brush. It was an old-fashioned remedy, but she had remained faithful to it for more than twenty years.

'Open your mouth.'

Before going to bed, he couldn't help going to look out of the window one last time before closing the shutters.

There was no one on the pavement opposite and the wind was blowing furiously, raising the dust along the reservation running down the centre of the boulevard.

He was sleeping so deeply that it took him a while to surface from his feverish slumber. Something alive was touching his arm insistently, and his reflex was to recoil.

It was a hand, which seemed to be trying to tell him something, and he pushed it away a second time and attempted to roll over.

'Maigret . . .'

His wife's voice was barely audible.

'He's here, on the landing. He didn't dare ring the bell, but he knocked gently. Can you hear me?'

'What?'

He stretched out his arm to switch on the bedside light and looked about him in surprise. What had he just been dreaming? He'd already forgotten, but he felt as if he were coming back from a very long way away, from another world.

'What did you say?'

'He's here. He knocked quietly on the door.'

Maigret got up and went to fetch his dressing gown from the armchair.

'What time is it?'

'Half past two.'

He picked up the pipe he hadn't finished when he went to bed and relit it.

'You're not afraid of—'

He turned on the light as he went into the sitting room, headed towards the front door, stood still for a moment and finally opened it.

The landing light on a time switch had long gone out and the man emerged from the shadows, illuminated by the lights from the apartment. He cast around for something to say. He must have prepared a lengthy speech, but, confronted by Maigret in a dressing gown, his hair tousled, just a couple of feet away, he was so overawed that all he could do was stammer:

'I'm disturbing you, aren't I?'

'Come in, Pigou.'

He could still dive down the stairs and flee, because he

was younger and more agile than Maigret. Once inside the apartment, it would be too late, and Maigret was careful to stay still, as with the squirrel.

Pigou wavered for what was probably only a few seconds, but it felt like an eternity. He stepped inside. Maigret thought briefly of locking the door and putting the key in his pocket, but he ended up shrugging.

'Aren't you cold?'

'The night isn't warm. The icy wind's the worst.'

'Sit down there. When you've warmed up you can take off your raincoat.'

He went to the bedroom door, and called from the passage to his wife, who was getting dressed:

'Make us two grogs.'

After which, relaxed, he sat down facing his visitor. At last he was seeing him close up. He had rarely been as curious about anyone as he was about this man.

What surprised him most was Pigou's youthful age. His round, slightly chubby face had something unfinished about it, something childlike.

'How old are you?'

'Forty-four.'

'You don't look it.'

'Did you ask for a grog for me?'

'For myself too. I've got flu, perhaps a throat infection, and it will do me good.'

'I don't normally drink, apart from a glass of wine with each meal. You find me dirty, don't you? I haven't been able to wash my clothes for a long time. The last time I had a wash in hot water was a week ago, in a public bathhouse in Rue Saint-Martin.'

They eyed each other while talking cagily.

'I was expecting you to come earlier.'

'Did you see me?'

'I even sensed that you were hesitating. You took a step forward, and then you went off in the direction of Rue du Chemin-Vert.'

'I could see your shape at the window. As I was in the dark, I didn't know whether you could see me, or, more importantly, recognize me.'

He started on hearing a noise, again like the squirrel. It was Madame Maigret bringing the grogs. She tactfully avoided staring at the visitor.

'A lot of sugar?'

'Yes, please.'

'Lemon?'

She prepared his drink and put the glass on the pedestal table in front of him. Then she served her husband.

'Call me if you need anything.'

'Who knows? Maybe another grog, later.'

It was obvious that Pigou was well-mannered and determined to behave properly. Glass in hand, he waited until Maigret took the first sip before drinking.

'It's scalding hot, but it does you good, doesn't it?'

'In any case, it will warm you up. Now you can take off your raincoat.'

He did so. His suit, which was not badly cut, was crumpled and had a few stains, including quite a large white paint stain.

Now, they couldn't think of anything to say. They both knew that when they spoke again, it would be to broach serious matters, and they were both reluctant to do so, for different reasons.

The silence lasted for a long time. They each took another sip of grog. Maigret got up to go and fill another pipe.

'Do you smoke?'

'I don't have any cigarettes left.'

There were some in the dresser drawer and Maigret offered them to his visitor. Flustered, Pigou looked at him as if he couldn't believe his eyes as Maigret brought a lighted match close to the cigarette.

They were both sitting down again and then Pigou said:

'Firstly, I must apologize for disturbing you at home, in the middle of the night to boot . . . I was afraid to come to Quai des Orfèvres. And I couldn't carry on walking alone through the streets of Paris.'

Maigret didn't miss a single expression on his face. In the privacy of the apartment, a grog within reach, his pipe in his mouth, he looked like a kind old man you could confide in.

# 7.

'What do you think of me?'

These were almost the first words he'd spoken and Maigret could tell that, for him, this question was capital. He must have been seeking the reply in people's eyes all his life.

How should he answer?

'I don't know you yet,' mumbled Maigret with a smile.

'Are you this kind to all criminals?'

'I can be very nasty too.'

'With what kind of people, for example?'

'Men like Oscar Chabut.'

All of a sudden, Pigou's eyes lit up, as if he'd just found an ally.

'You know, it's true that I stole a little money from him. Barely what he spent each month on tips. But he was the real thief. He stole my dignity and my manly pride. He humiliated me to the point where I was almost ashamed to be alive.'

'What gave you the idea of helping yourself from petty cash?'

'I have to tell you everything, don't I?'

'Otherwise there would be no point in your coming here.'

'You've seen my wife. What do you think of her?'

'I don't know her very well. She got married so that she could give up her job and I'm surprised she carried on working for three years.'

'Two and a half years.'

'She is one of those women who want to live a nice, cosy little life.'

'You guessed that?'

'It's very obvious.'

'Often, in the evenings, I was the one who had to do the housework. If I'd listened to her, we'd have eaten out every night to save her the effort of cooking. I don't think it's her fault. She's lethargic. Her sisters are like her.'

'Do they live in Paris?'

'One is in Algiers, married to a petroleum engineer. Another lives in Marseille and has three children.'

'Why don't you have children?'

'I would have liked to, but Liliane categorically refused to have any.'

'I understand.'

'She has a third sister and a brother who—'

He shook his head.

'What's the use of talking about all that. It sounds as if I'm trying to avoid taking full responsibility.'

He took a sip of rum and lit a second cigarette.

'I'm keeping you up, at this hour—'

'Go on. Your wife also humiliated you.'

'How do you know?'

'She reprimanded you for not earning enough, didn't she?'

'She was forever saying that she wondered how she could have married me.

'Then she'd sigh:

' "To spend my entire life in a one-bedroom apartment and with no cleaning woman!" '

He seemed to be talking to himself. He didn't look at Maigret but stared at a corner of the rug.

'Was she unfaithful?'

'Yes. From the first year of our marriage. I only found out two or three years later. One day, I'd had to leave the office early to go to the dentist, and I saw her on the arm of a man, near the Madeleine church, and the pair of them went into a hotel.'

'Did you speak to her about it?'

'Yes. But she was the one who heaped abuse on me. I wasn't providing the sort of life a young woman could expect. In the evenings, I was sleepy and she almost had to drag me by force to the cinema. Home truths like that. Including that I didn't satisfy her sexually . . .'

He had blushed at those last words and that accusation must have been the most painful of all.

'One day, on her birthday, three years ago, I dipped into the till just for the money to pay for a good dinner, and I took her to a restaurant on the Grands Boulevards.

' "I think I'm about to get a rise," I told her.

' "About time too. Your boss ought to be ashamed to be paying you so little. If I were to go and see him, I'd give him a piece of my mind." '

'You only took small amounts?'

'Yes. At first, I said I'd received an increase of fifty francs a month. She soon found that wasn't enough and I gave myself a rise, so to speak, of a hundred francs.'

'Weren't you afraid of being found out?'

'It had become a habit. No one audited my books. It was such a small thing amid all the machinery of the company's finances!'

'Once, you took a five-hundred-franc note.'

'It was for Christmas. I said I'd been given a bonus. I almost ended up believing it myself. It boosted my self-respect.

'You see, I've never had a high opinion of myself. My father would have liked me to work at the Crédit Lyonnais like him, but I'd have had to suffer the comparison with people who are much cleverer than me. At Quai de Charenton, I worked quietly in my corner and no one ever really took any notice of me.'

'How did Chabut discover your cheating?'

'He wasn't the one who found out, it was Monsieur Louceck. He'd come in from time to time and check my figures. Something must have made him suspicious. Instead of talking to me about it, he acted as though nothing was amiss and informed Monsieur Chabut.'

'Was that in June?'

'The end of June, yes. The twenty-eighth of June. I'll never forget it. He sent for me to go up to his office. The secretary was there and he didn't ask her to leave. I wasn't worried because it didn't occur to me that I'd been found out.'

'He asked you to sit down.'

'Yes. How do you know?'

'The Grasshopper – I mean Anne-Marie – told me what happened. After a few minutes, she was as mortified as you were.'

'And I was mortified at being trampled on in front of a woman. He chose the most contemptuous, most hurtful words. I would far rather he'd called in the police.

'You could have sworn he was enjoying himself. Each time I thought it was over, he was off again, even more violently. Do you know what annoyed him the most? That I only filched tiny amounts.

'He said that he'd have respected a genuine thief, but not a small-time pilferer.'

He was quiet for a moment while he got his breath back, because he had just spoken with some vehemence and his face had turned crimson. He took another sip. Maigret did likewise.

'When he ordered me to come closer, I didn't have the least idea what he was going to do but, even so, I was afraid. The slap arrived with full force and the marks from his fingers must have remained imprinted on my cheek for a long time.

'I had never been slapped. Even when I was a kid, my parents didn't hit me. I stood there, indecisive, without reacting, and he shouted something like:

' "And now, get out of here . . ."'

'I can't remember whether it was at that point or just before that he told me that he wouldn't give me a reference and that he'd ensure I wouldn't be able to find a decent job.'

'He too was humiliated,' murmured Maigret very softly.

Pigou turned abruptly towards him, open-mouthed in surprise.

'He actually said to you that no one mocked him with impunity.'

'That's true. I hadn't understood that that was the underlying reason for his attitude. Do you think he was offended?'

'More than offended. He was a strong man, a man who thought of himself as strong, in any case, who had succeeded in everything he did. Don't forget that he'd started out as a door-to-door encyclopaedia salesman.

'For him, you barely existed. You soldiered on in a ground-floor room where he almost never set foot, and it was a little like a favour he was doing by keeping you on.'

'Yes, that's definitely him.'

'He too needed to boost his ego and that's why he seduced every woman he met.'

Gilbert Pigou raised his eyebrows, suddenly anxious.

'Do you mean he was to be pitied?'

'We are all to be pitied in some way. I try to understand. My aim is not to decide each person's share of blame. You left Quai de Charenton. Where did you go first of all?'

'It was eleven o'clock in the morning. I was never out and about at that hour. It was very hot. I walked in the shade of the plane trees along by the Bercy warehouses, I went into a bar, near the Pont d'Austerlitz, and I drank two or three brandies, I can't remember.'

'Did you have lunch with your wife?'

'She'd long since stopped coming to meet me at midday. I walked a lot, I drank a lot, and at some point I went into a cinema where it was a little cooler than outside, because my shirt was plastered to my skin. June was torrid, do you remember?'

He gave the impression he didn't want to omit the tiniest detail. He needed to give an account of himself and, since he was being allowed to, because Maigret was listening to him with obvious interest, he tried not to leave anything unexplained.

'That evening, did your wife not notice you'd been drinking?'

'I told her that my colleagues had bought me a drink because I'd just been promoted and had been to the office in Avenue de l'Opéra.'

Maigret did not smile at this naivety and, on the contrary, his face was solemn.

'How did you manage, two days later, to give your wife your month's pay?'

'I didn't have any savings. She gave me just forty francs a month for my cigarettes and my Métro tickets. I had to find something. I thought about it nearly all night. On leaving, I told her I wouldn't be home for dinner because I'd be spending part of the evening moving into my new office.

'The previous day, I hadn't thought to give back the key to the safe. I knew it must contain more cash than usual because the next day was pay day.

'Over the years, I'd sometimes go back to the office in the evening when there was urgent work to be done. I'd take home the key to the main door.

'Once, I forgot it. I walked round the building, remembering that the back door was warped and didn't close properly and you could jiggle the bolt with a penknife.'

'Wasn't there a security guard?'

'No. I waited until dark and slipped into the yard. The little door opened as I'd hoped and I went into my former office. I took a wad of bills, without counting.'

'Was it a large amount?'

'More than three months' salary. That night, I hid the money above the big wardrobe, except my month's pay. I left at the same time as usual. I couldn't tell Liliane that I'd been fired.'

'Why were you so worried about what she might think of you?'

'Because she was a sort of witness. For years, she watched me with a critical eye. I wanted there to be one person at least who believed in me.

'I started spending my days on the streets, looking for a new job. I'd imagined that it would be easy. I read the classified ads and I raced over to the addresses given. Sometimes men were queueing and occasionally I felt sorry for some of them. They were nearly all old and they waited without hope.

'I was asked questions. The first one was always about my age. When I replied "forty-five", that was usually the end of the interview.

' "We're looking for a young man, no older than thirty."

'I thought I was young. I felt young. I grew gloomier by the day. After two weeks, I no longer sought a position as a book-keeper necessarily and I'd have been happy with a job as office boy or sales assistant in a department store.

'At best, they made a note of my name and address:

' "We'll write to you."

'Those who were considering the possibility of hiring me asked where I'd worked previously. After Chabut's threats, I didn't dare tell them.

' "Here and there. I lived abroad for a long time."

'I had to add that it was in Belgium, or Switzerland, because I spoke only French.

' "Do you have references?"

' "I'll forward them to you."

'Of course, I didn't go back to those companies.

'At the end of July, it was worse. A lot of offices were

closed, or the bosses were on holiday. Again I took my pay home, or rather I took the corresponding sum from my stash on top of the wardrobe.

' "You've been strange, recently," my wife said. "You seem more tired than when you were at Quai de Charenton."

' "Because I'm not used to my new job yet. I have to learn to work with computers. At Avenue de l'Opéra, we are in charge of the sales outlets and there are more than fifteen thousand of them. That means I have heavy responsibilities."

' "When will you have your holiday?"

' "I won't have time to take any this year. Maybe at Christmas? It would be nice to go on a winter break for the first time. But you can go away. Why not go and spend three or four weeks with your family?" '

Was he aware how tragic, how wretched, his words sounded?

'She went away for a month. She spent two weeks at her parents' place, in Aix-en-Provence, where her father is an architect, then two weeks in a villa in Bandol, rented by one of her sisters, the one who has three children.

'I felt very lost in Paris. I carried on reading the job ads in Rue Réaumur and I hurried over to the addresses given. Still with as little success.

'I began to realize that Chabut was right, that I would never find any kind of job.

'I went and hung around his home, in Place des Vosges, for no reason, just to get a glimpse of him, but he was on holiday too, in Cannes, most likely, where they have an apartment.'

'Did you hate him?'

'Yes. With every fibre of my being. It felt unjust that he should be lying in the sun while I was trying to find a job in an increasingly empty Paris.

'All I had left on top of the wardrobe was enough to give my wife one more month's pay.

'And then what? What would I do after that? I would have to tell her the truth, and I was certain she'd leave me. She wasn't the sort of woman to stay with me if I wasn't able to fulfil her needs.'

'Were you still fond of her?'

'I think so. I don't know.'

'What about now?'

'I feel as if she's gradually become a stranger. I'm surprised it mattered so much to me what she might think.'

'When was the last time you saw her?'

'She came back from the South at the end of August. I gave her what was supposedly my pay. I stayed with her for nearly three weeks, but I already knew I wouldn't have enough money at the end of the month.

'One morning, I left with the idea of not coming back, so I didn't take anything with me, other than the few hundred francs I had left.'

'Did you go straight to Rue de la Grande-Truanderie?'

'You know about that? No. I took a room in a cheap but still decent hotel and I chose the Bastille neighbourhood, where there was no danger of running into my wife.'

'Is that when you started following Oscar Chabut?'

'I knew where he was at such-and-such a time and I hung around Avenue de l'Opéra, Place des Vosges or Quai de Charenton. I was also aware that, nearly every Wednesday, he went to Rue Fortuny with his secretary.'

'What was your intention?'

'I didn't have one. He was the man who'd played the most important role in my life, because he'd stripped me of all my dignity and of any chance of getting back on my feet.'

'Were you armed?'

Pigou pulled a small, blue-coloured automatic from his trouser pocket, stood up and went over to place it on the pedestal table in front of Maigret.

'I'd taken it with me in case I felt the urge to commit suicide.'

'You didn't try to?'

'I did, several times, especially at night, but I was too afraid. I've always been scared of blows, of physical pain. Perhaps Chabut was right: I'm a coward.'

'I must interrupt you for a moment to make a telephone call. You will understand why.'

He called Quai des Orfèvres.

'Put me through to Inspector Lapointe, please, mademoiselle . . .'

Pigou opened his mouth to speak but said nothing.

In the kitchen, Madame Maigret was making some more grog.

# 8.

'Is that you?' asked Maigret.

'Aren't you in bed, chief? You don't even sound like some-one who's just woken up. I haven't received any reports.'

'I know.'

'How can you know? Where are you phoning me from?'

'From my place.'

'It's three o'clock in the morning.'

'You can call all the men off. Their surveillance is over.'

'Have you found him?'

'He's here, sitting opposite me, and the two of us are having a quiet chat.'

'Did he come of his own accord?'

'I can't see me chasing him down Boulevard Richard-Lenoir.'

'How is he?'

'Fine.'

'Do you need me?'

'Not yet but stay at the office. Call off the various patrols. Inform Janvier, Lucas, Torrence and Lourtie. I'll phone you later.'

He hung up and remained silent while Madame Maigret replaced the empty glasses with full ones.

'I forgot to tell you, Pigou, that although we're in my home and not at Quai des Orfèvres, I am still a police officer and I reserve the right to use anything you might tell me.'

'That's natural.'

'Do you know a good lawyer?'

'No. Not any good or bad lawyers.'

'You'll need one tomorrow, when you are interviewed by the examining magistrate. I'll give you some names.'

'Thank you.'

The telephone call had rather dampened the mood, which now became more awkward.

'To your health.'

'To yours.'

And Pigou joked:

'I don't think I'll be drinking a grog again for a long time. They're going to crucify me, aren't they?'

'Why would they crucify you?'

'One, because he was a rich and influential man. Two, because I can't even give a reason.'

'When did it occur to you to kill him?'

'I don't know. First of all, I had to leave my hotel near Bastille and that was when I went to Rue de la Grande-Truanderie. It was very hard. After unloading vegetables at Les Halles, I'd come back at daybreak and cry myself to sleep. The smell made me feel sick and even the hotel noises. I felt an outcast, as if I was in a different world.

'During the day, I'd still sometimes hang around Place des Vosges, Quai de Charenton or Avenue de l'Opéra and, a couple of times, I even went and hid in the Montparnasse cemetery and spied on Liliane.

'Whenever I spotted Chabut, more and more frequently I'd mumble to myself:

' "I'm going to kill him."

'They were just words that came out of my mouth

automatically. I didn't really intend to kill him. From a distance, I watched him living, so to speak. I saw his big red car, his face oozing self-assurance, his beautifully tailored clothes without a single crease.

'Whereas I was going downhill fast. The only suit I'd taken with me from Rue Froidevaux was more and more crumpled and covered in stains. My raincoat didn't protect me from the cold, but I couldn't afford to buy a coat, not even from a second-hand clothes shop.

'I was on the embankment, some distance away, when I saw Liliane go into the offices at Quai de Charenton. She had probably been to Avenue de l'Opéra first, because that was where I was supposed to be working.

'She stayed there for some time. At one point, I saw Anne-Marie come out for a breath of air in the yard, and I could guess what was going on.

'I wasn't jealous. It was just like one more slap in the face. That man behaved as if the whole world belonged to him. Again, I muttered:

' "I'm going to kill him!"

'I limped away. I didn't want to be seen by my wife.'

'When did you go to Rue Fortuny for the first time?'

'Around the end of November. I even had to save for Métro tickets.'

He gave a bitter little laugh.

'It's a strange feeling, you know, not to have any money in your pocket and to know you will never again live like other people. At Les Halles, you meet mainly old men, but there are a few young ones too, who already have the same look in their eyes. Do I have that look?'

'No.'

'I ought to, because I became like them. But I still brooded over that slap. He was wrong to hit me. I might have forgotten the words, even the most contemptuous, the most demeaning. But he slapped me as if I were a naughty brat.'

'Last Wednesday, when you went to Rue Fortuny, did you know that it would be for the last time?'

'There would be no point my coming here, would there, if it wasn't to tell the truth. I didn't know I was going to kill him, I swear, and you can believe me. I wouldn't lie to you.'

'What was your state of mind?'

'I felt this couldn't go on. I had reached rock bottom. Sooner or later I'd be picked up in a police raid, or I'd fall ill and be taken to hospital. Something had to happen.'

'What, for example?'

'I could have returned his slap. If he came out of the building with Anne-Marie, I would walk towards him . . .'

He shook his head.

'That wasn't possible, because he was much stronger than me. I waited until nine o'clock. I saw the light go on in the entrance and he came out alone. My automatic was still in my pocket, but I whipped it out in an instant.

'I fired without really aiming, three or four times, I don't remember.'

'Four.'

'My initial thought was to stay put and wait for the police. But I was afraid of being beaten and I began to run towards the Métro on Avenue de Villiers. No one chased me. I found myself back in Les Halles and I mechanically signed up to lug vegetables. I couldn't have stayed in my room on my own.

'There, inspector. I think I've told you everything.'

'Why did you telephone me?'

'I don't know. I felt alone and I didn't think anyone would ever understand me. I've often read about you in the newspapers. I wanted to meet you. I'd more or less decided to blow my brains out.

'So I tried to make contact one last time, but I was still scared, not of you, but of your officers.'

'My inspectors don't beat anyone up.'

'But people say they do.'

'People say a lot of things, Pigou. You may light your cigarette. Are you still afraid?'

'No. I telephoned you a second time, then, almost immediately afterwards, I wrote to you from a café on Boulevard du Palais. I felt close to you. I wanted to follow you in the street, but I couldn't because you were always in a car. I had the same problem with Chabut.

'I had to be one step ahead of you, to guess in advance where you were planning to go.

'That's how I was there when you went to Quai de Charenton. It was inevitable that Anne-Marie would talk to you. It didn't even occur to me that she wouldn't on your first visit.

'It's true that the scene took place in June and that, for her, it was already ancient history.

'I saw you at Place des Vosges too.'

'And Quai des Orfèvres.'

'Yes. I told myself there was no point hiding because I was bound to be caught. Because you would soon have arrested me, wouldn't you?'

'If you'd stayed in Les Halles, you'd probably have been

identified and arrested tonight. At ten o'clock they found the Hôtel du Cygne and they would most likely have come across you, during the night, in one of the bars in the street. Have you started to drink?'

'No.'

It was rare for someone to fall so far and not take to drink.

'I almost walked into Quai des Orfèvres and asked to speak to you. Then I thought they'd put me in the hands of some inspector or other and I wouldn't get the chance to meet you. So I came to Boulevard Richard-Lenoir.'

'I saw you.'

'I saw you too. My plan was to come up to your apartment. I could see you silhouetted in the window, with the light behind you, and, in your dressing gown, you looked enormous. I panicked and ran away fast. I skulked around the neighbourhood for hours. I walked past your place more than five times even though the lights in your apartment were off.'

'Would you excuse me for a moment?'

He dialled the number of Quai des Orfèvres.

'Put me through to Lapointe, please. Hello! Have the men gone home? Who's there with you?'

'Lucas is on duty. Janvier's just arrived.'

'Both of you are to come over to my place. Bring a car.'

'Are they going to take me away?' asked Pigou when Maigret hung up.

'They have to.'

'I understand, but I'm still scared. It's like going to the dentist's.'

He had killed a man. He had come to Maigret's home

of his own free will, but his overriding feeling was fear. Fear of being beaten, of violence.

He barely alluded to his crime.

Maigret recalled the young Stiernet, who had killed his grandmother with multiple blows from a poker, and it wouldn't have been surprising to hear him say:

'*I didn't do it on purpose.*'

He gazed intently at Pigou, as if trying to look deep into his soul. The book-keeper was troubled by that gaze.

'Do you have any questions for me?' he asked.

'No, I don't think so.'

What was the point of asking him if he regretted his action in Rue Fortuny? Did Stiernet regret having struck his grandmother?

He would most likely be asked the question at his trial and, if he answered truthfully, there would be various reactions, even a disapproving murmur from the courtroom.

They sat there for a long time in silence, and Maigret drained his glass. Then he heard a car draw up outside the building, one door slamming and then another.

He lit a last pipe, more for the sake of appearances than from a desire to smoke. There were footsteps on the stairs. He went to open the door. The two men peered curiously into the sitting room where the light formed a bluish glow around the lamp and the ceiling light.

'Gilbert Pigou. We have just had a long conversation. Tomorrow we'll proceed with the official questioning.'

The book-keeper looked at them, somewhat reassured by their behaviour. They didn't seem like men who beat people up.

'Take him to Quai des Orfèvres and let him sleep for a few hours. I'll be there by late morning.'

Lapointe gave a signal which Maigret didn't understand at first because he was exhausted. He was indicating his wrists, which of course meant:

'Do I handcuff him?'

Maigret turned to Pigou.

'It's not because they distrust you,' he murmured. 'They'll remove them when you get to Quai des Orfèvres. It's the rule.'

On the landing, Pigou turned around. He had tears in his eyes. He looked at Maigret one more time, as if to draw strength.

But was he not just feeling sorry for himself?

# OTHER TITLES IN THE SERIES

## MAIGRET IN VICHY
GEORGES SIMENON

*'What else did they have to do with their days? They ambled around casually. From time to time, they paused, not because they were out of breath, but to admire a tree, a house, the play of light and shadow, or a face.'*

While taking a much-needed rest cure in Vichy with his wife, Maigret feels compelled to help with a local investigation, unravelling the secrets of the spa town's elegant inhabitants.

Translated by Ros Schwartz

## OTHER TITLES IN THE SERIES

### MAIGRET'S CHILDHOOD FRIEND
GEORGES SIMENON

'*Florentin pulled one of those faces which had once amused his classmates so much and disarmed the teachers . . .*

*Maigret didn't dare to ask why he had come to see him. He studied him, struggling to believe that so many years had passed . . .*

*He was so used to acting the fool that his face automatically assumed comical expressions. But his face was still greyish, his eyes anxious.*'

A visit from a long-lost schoolmate who has fallen on hard times forces Maigret to unpick a seedy tangle of love affairs in Montmartre, and to confront the tragedy of a wasted life.

Translated by Shaun Whiteside

# Other Titles in the Series

## MAIGRET AND THE KILLER
GEORGES SIMENON

'Leaning on the banisters, Madame Maigret watched her husband going heavily downstairs . . . what the newspapers didn't know was how much energy he put into trying to understand, how much he concentrated during certain investigations. It was as if he identified with the people he was hunting and suffered the same torments as they did.'

A young man is found dead, clutching his tape recorder, just streets away from Maigret's home, leading the inspector on a disturbing trail into the mind of a killer.

Translated by Shaun Whiteside

# OTHER TITLES IN THE SERIES

www.penguin.com